DRACONIS

LARRY RHODES

Published in the United States of America

Brilliant Books Literary
137 Forest Park Lane Thomasville
North Carolina 27360 USA

ISBN:
Paperback: 979-8-88945-385-7
Ebook: 979-8-88945-386-4
Hardback: 979-8-88945-387-1

Chapter 1

CNEOS DISCOVERY

Mary Gordon yawned and sipped slowly on a cup of hot coffee as she stared at a 3D computer simulation of known objects in near Earth orbit. This was just another boring Thursday evening at the Jet Propulsion Laboratory's Center for Near Earth Objects Studies (CNEOS) monitoring facility. The NEO database had just been updated with some newly identified objects greater than the 140 meters diameter threshold for inclusion in the database, and the computer simulation was updating its 3D graphic display to include the new objects.

Her cell phone rang, and she glanced at the caller ID. She frowned as it was her colleague and former boyfriend in London calling. She glanced at her watch and shook her head. Just after 6 PM meant it was 2 AM there. She hoped it wasn't another story about UFOs. How could an astrophysicist with such a bright future spend so much of his free time chasing down eyewitness accounts of UFOs?

"Hi, Mike. Isn't it 2AM there? What's going on?"

"Mary, you're not going to believe what was found today in London."

"I hope this isn't some more UFO crap."

"Crap? No, a small silver electronic device was found with some strange markings on it that no one can figure out."

"Someone probably planted it there to make you and your fellow UFO guys look like idiots."

"I knew you'd say that, so I just sent a picture of it to you."

Gordon opened the email and stared at a picture of a small silver tube about the size of a tube of lipstick.

"It was found by some construction guys who were remodeling an old Victorian era brownstone. The architect of the renovation is a friend of mine."

"Okay, so what's the big deal?"

"It was found behind a huge old armoire. It had probably rolled behind it and whoever dropped it probably couldn't move the armoire to get it. There was some other stuff that had fallen back there over time and the silver cylinder was underneath a newspaper. Guess what year the newspaper was from."

"Five or ten years ago…"

"No, it was from 1900. Think of it, a tiny audio recording device older than 1900!"

Mary frowned. "How do you know it's a recording device?"

"It still works. There are some indentations on it, and you can operate the device by pressing on the indentations. I just sent you a video."

"Wait, it still works?" Mary received a shaky cell phone video and heard someone speaking in a totally unknown language. "Does this mean there are tiny batteries in it that are over a hundred years old and they're still working?

"I don't know what kind of power source it has. That's why I called you. We're trying to find someone who can open it and help us figure it out."

"Okay, make a clear video of it working and I'll find someone who might be able to help."

"Uh, I can't. I was hoping that video was good enough."

"Why not?"

"The new owner of the brownstone somehow found out about it and came to the architect's office this evening to reclaim it. He said everything found on the property is his. We want to go to him and convince him to let us test it, so we need to know how to open it."

Mary suddenly laughed. "You almost had me on that one. Another tall tale with unsubstantiated evidence again. Like all your other UFO stories." Mike's obsession with UFOs and the time, money, and effort he put into it, had ultimately led to their breakup.

"No, I swear it's true. Look at the video again."

"Bye, Mike."

"Don't leave the call!"

Mary ended the call just as her computer simulation update was interrupted by an audible alarm with a flashing red warning notice on the computer screen of an impending meteor strike on the Earth. She quickly cleared the alarm, assuming it was a computer glitch as no ground-based telescope organizations had given any notice of a new approach of a meteor strike on Earth in more than a year. The alarm returned, and Mary called a colleague at the Pan-STARRS observatory on top of the Haleakala volcano in Maui, Hawaii to confirm the impending danger. Jonas Schmidt had just verified the threat and commented the observatory had not previously seen the meteors as they were in a tightly clustered swarm and very small in size. The Pan-STARRS computers had also just confirmed the meteors would barely miss the Earth and because they were so small, would have only a minimal effect on telecommunications or the national power grid. He even suggested the impending meteor strike might even produce a better light show than the famous Perseid meteor shower.

Mary breathed a huge sigh of relief. As she sat there waiting for the program to finish updating the model, she was interrupted by a cell phone call with "Arun Patel" on the Caller ID, her current boyfriend.

After a brief exchange on when she could come home for a late dinner, she changed the subject to describe the meteor shower that was imminent. She knew that Arun couldn't stop talking about the last time he saw the Perseid meteor shower. She was surprised, and somewhat annoyed, when Arun said he was going to visit a friend in Texas and would probably watch the meteor shower there, before coming back.

The next day news organizations began reporting the impending meteor event as a fabulous light show. Astrophysicists were soon arguing with the International Meteor Society over the name of the meteor shower as it appeared to originate in the Draco constellation. Previous meteor showers, known as Draconids, and originating from that star system usually occurred in October. This was three months later and after a lot of heated discussions they agreed on the modified name "January Draconids." One TV reporter snarked that "Draco" is Latin for Dragon and joked that Earth was about to be attacked by Dragons.

One newspaper chain erroneously misspelled the meteor shower as Draconis and it was soon picked up by other organizations and went viral on social media especially among video game and fantasy movie enthusiasts, until most people were now referring to the meteor shower as just "Draconis".

One day before the meteor shower would be visible from the ground without a telescope, the NEO computers updated their prediction of the paths of the small meteor shower and Mary rubbed her eyes in disbelief. The prediction confirmed the impending meteor cluster would barely miss the Earth, but the meteors paths were beginning to diverge, and the flybys would virtually cover the surface of the Earth. That was impossible.

Chapter 2

DRACONIS METEOR SHOWER

Tomas Cordoba returned from a quick bathroom break to his operator's console at the South Texas Nuclear Generating Facility. A veteran of almost 20 years, he knew the operation of the water treatment unit like the back of his hand. His immediate supervisor, Mike Tomkins, wandered over. After a brief exchange on the current operation of the water treating equipment, Mike turned to leave then stopped and looked back.

"Are you going to watch the Draconis meteor shower tonight?"

That jogged Tomas' memory. This meteor shower was supposed to be much more spectacular than the famous Perseid meteor shower. "What time was that supposed to start?"

"Just after midnight when your shift ends."

"Uh, yeah, it might be interesting."

At the end of his shift, Tomas changed clothes and went outside to see if the Draconis meteor shower would live up to its hype. At first, he didn't see anything then the most spectacular light show he had ever seen began. Not only did the meteors streak brightly across the sky, but they seemed to leave a thick trail of sparkling particles in their wake. It was truly spectacular. Too bad his cell phone camera couldn't take decent nighttime pictures. Maybe his wife could take some? He tried to call her several times but couldn't connect. He also tried to call several friends to take pictures of the meteors but couldn't connect with them either. He wondered if the meteor shower could be affecting the cell phone system.

As he headed to his truck, he noticed a few tiny shimmering particles falling to the ground around him. He had never seen or heard of tiny particles from meteors falling to the Earth. He also noticed an unusual smell. It seemed somewhat like the smell of antiseptics in a hospital. He shrugged it off and as he neared his truck, he saw three workers pulling cans of beers from an ice chest in the back of their car. They all started drinking and staring at the amazing light show overhead. One even toasted the meteor shower. "Draconis!" The others laughed not noticing the tiny dust particles floating down on them and everything in the parking lot.

The next day Tomas had to call maintenance when one of the wastewater pumps started acting up. When that minor emergency was resolved he sat back in his chair and stared at the video monitors over his operating console. His eyes glazed over as he stared at the monitors wondering what they were for. He looked down at the operating console and it all seemed like a maze of small screens, buttons, and switches. What did it mean? What was he supposed to do? An alarm sounded, and a red light blinked at him. He became more and more confused and just sat there wondering what he should do, until Mike walked by, heard the alarm, and noticed Tomas staring off into space.

"Hey, Tomas, is everything okay?"

Tomas glanced at him. He knew he should know the person who was asking him a question, but just couldn't remember who he was.

Mike shook his shoulder. "Tomas! Are you okay?"

Tomas just stared at him, and Mike went to find someone who could take over Tomas' operating position. He also called the medical department and asked them to find out why Tomas was just staring off into space.

Later that day, the site's nurse practitioner sent Tomas home to rest and Mike filled out a report describing the day's events. When Tomas returned to his house, his wife Suzanne was gone, and a note lay on the kitchen table. Suzanne had taken their children Ana and Camila to her mom's until he returned home as she would be gone for a few days to Costa Rica looking for a meteor from the prior night's meteor shower. She was a geologist by training, but her passion was finding celestial objects that fell to earth, studying them and writing scientific papers describing her findings. She was an assistant professor and needed to be published in as many journals as possible, if she ever wanted to be promoted to associate professor and then to a full, tenured professor.

Suzanne Cordoba wiped the sweat from her eyes. She was suffering from the summer like heat and humidity of Costa Rica in January. She had been hired by a wealthy collector to find what was believed to be the only meteor in the recent meteor shower to impact the earth, somewhere near the base of the Arenal Volcano in Costa Rica. Perhaps she would be lucky, and the meteor had impacted higher up the volcano where the heat and humidity were not as suffocating.

She had been given GPS coordinates by her wealthy benefactor, who had secretly paid an enormous sum of money to a NASA Near Earth Object Studies insider for the approximate coordinates of the impact. She had to get this done quickly. Many other agencies and societies would have the same information and would undoubtedly be sending searchers as well.

The first evidence of the "event" was the loss of a communication satellite. Preliminary data indicated one of the small meteors had grazed the satellite, pulling it out of orbit and dragging it as it hurtled toward Earth. Maybe Suzanne would be lucky and find satellite fragments as well as meteor fragments. Her benefactor would be happy with the meteor fragments. He hadn't mentioned recovery of the satellite fragments. She knew people had paid dearly in the past whenever something fell from orbit or from space and fragments were recovered. Maybe she could write a scientific paper AND collect the reward for the meteor fragments before she sold or donated the satellite fragments.

She took a break from her trek for a drink of water and glanced up at the volcano when she felt the ground tremble and heard a rumbling noise that sounded like thunder. Arenal was an active volcano and the rumbling noise near the summit was not thunder but the sound of large rocks rolling down the sides. She smelled something different than the flora and fauna she had been trekking through for two days. What was that? It had a distinct chemical smell, almost like an antiseptic in a hospital. When she looked down, she spotted a palm-sized shiny object and picked it up. Metallic and triangular, it was definitively not natural. It wasn't very thick, and the sides were full of tiny holes, almost like a sponge. Perhaps it was a part of the satellite? Even as she held the triangular piece it began to slowly break apart into many smaller triangular pieces until there was only dust in her hand. She suddenly realized there were similar pieces all over the ground and yelled to her trek assistants to bring the boxes they were carrying. Together they quickly filled three small boxes with the shiny pieces. Surely, many pieces of the satellite would be worth a great deal of money to a collector of space debris. Now, where was the meteor?

Her companions continued picking up metal pieces while she left to find the meteor. When she came to a small clearing, she could see a definite crater surrounded by charred vegetation and hurried as quickly as she could toward the partially dirt-covered mass in the crater. When she finally neared the object she stopped, took her cap off and wiped the sweat from her eyes. What was going on? The mass had obviously burned extensively in its passage through the atmosphere, but she could easily make out the shape of a satellite from the remains. She would need a bigger box and perhaps a few more helpers to bring something this large back with her.

Then it dawned on her. If this was the satellite, where was the meteor and what were all the small shiny triangular metal pieces? They didn't even appear to be burned or charred. Her workers finally caught up with her and she told them to find a container large enough for the satellite. They replied it might be too heavy to transport back to their village. She told them to find more helpers in the village if necessary.

When they left, she looked carefully at the large cache of shiny triangular metal pieces the workers had gathered. Was that a blue powder on the edges of several of the pieces? She wiped her finger on one of them and then gazed at the blue powder on her finger. What could that be? She sneezed and realized the blue powder was now a fine mist above the open box. She quickly put a top on the box and sat down to wait for the worker's return.

When they returned, she was staring off into space and they had to shake her to get her attention. She stared at them for a moment wondering who they were and what they wanted until they started using poles as levers to move the satellite remains onto a large cart with wheels. Her memory returned, and she checked the area around the satellite impact site for any fragments typical of a meteor.

Chapter 3

PRESS CONFERENCE

Barely a week had passed since Suzanne Cordoba had returned from Costa Rica with the remains of the satellite and the three small boxes of shiny metallic pieces, she assumed were fragments of the meteor. Word of her discovery had somehow leaked to the press and suddenly there was a huge tug of war between several governments and corporations over the rights to the satellite and the meteor. She knew that fallen meteorites generally belong to the landowner while fallen satellites generally belong to the countries that put them in space. This was complicated by the fact that a meteor had knocked a satellite out of orbit, so there were many legal issues to be settled.

After photographing and examining the satellite carefully, she gave it up to the university to lead the fight over the ultimate rights to it as the university was among a number of entities claiming some rights to it. The purported meteor fragments were an even bigger story as she was shocked when her university arranged a press conference for her to talk about the satellite and the possible meteor fragments, she found in Costa Rica. She hadn't even had time to examine the meteor fragments properly.

She used rubber gloves, inside a protective air handling hood, to transfer a few of the metal fragments from one of the boxes to a plastic container and sent it to the science department to have X-Ray and non-destructive metals analyses done. They barely had time to run preliminary tests before the press conference. Suzanne was literally handed the results of the tests as she was being introduced to the press.

She stared in disbelief at the results – the metal was unidentifiable, which she read to be not of Earth origin. This was the worst possible case for a geologist (or any scientist) as it made it look like she was saying the pieces were manufactured but not on Earth. She had visions of her name tied to UFOs or aliens or some other conspiracy theories that could effectively end her career as a geologist.

As she walked to the podium, she noticed some of the meteor fragments were displayed on a table next to the podium and someone had transferred them from the boxes to large clear plastic bags. She hoped whoever did that was wearing protective respirator gear. Several reporters and photographers were gathered around the fragments, discussing their origin, and photographing them. She even heard one reporter wonder out loud if this was all a big hoax.

Suzanne began her statement by describing the hard trek up the volcano in Costa Rica in search of the satellite remains and stumbling across the displayed pieces by accident. She couldn't say for sure that these were fragments of the meteor that had struck the satellite, sending both to the Earth, but she confirmed that after an extensive search of the area no other artifacts could be found that were not natural to the area or the volcano.

When asked how she was able to beat numerous other teams of searchers to the possible satellite and meteor impact sites, she only said she had been given the likely coordinates by a benefactor who funded her trip and wished to remain anonymous.

When a reporter asked if the university had performed any analyses of the possible meteor fragments, she could only read them the X-Ray and metal analyses results.

Her worse nightmare came true when a reporter asked if she was suggesting these shiny triangular shaped objects were not manufactured on Earth. Before she could answer that, she noticed the photographers bumping into each other to obtain better pictures and cautioned them to be careful as there was a fine blue dust on the pieces that hadn't been examined yet that seemed to cause memory issues if inhaled. She then described her own memory lapse when she had picked up several of the pieces from the ground.

As she was about to answer the question on the fragment's possible origin, a photographer's shoulder bag accidentally bumped into one of the plastic bags, knocking it to the floor where it burst open. The fragments inside shattered and everyone nearby could see the fine blue dust Suzanne had just described. Those nearest the fragments yelled to the rest which set off a panic evacuation of the room. Suzanne saw the photographer who had knocked the plastic bag to the floor stoop over and try to put the pieces back into the bag. He suddenly stood up, staring off into space. Suzanne covered her nose and mouth with her hand and ran for the press room's back door.

Suzanne had warned the scientists in the metals analysis lab of the possible issues with the fine blue powder. They appreciated her warning but said they would be following standard procedures for examining hazardous samples of unknown origin and were wearing protective clothing and face masks as they examined the fragments. They were fascinated to watch the larger shiny pieces in their Nitrile-gloved hands seemingly crumble into much smaller triangular metal pieces. They also noticed the very act of breaking apart seemed to result in a fine blue mist of powder that was now on their protective clothing and masks. Per the biohazard protocol, the lab had a negative atmospheric pressure relative to the rest of the building that should prevent anything in the room from escaping and contaminating the other labs.

While all this was interesting, the results of their first tests were shocking and somewhat disturbing as the X-Ray and metals analysis software system could not identify the fragments composition. They carefully collected some of the blue dust and sent it to the Centers for Disease Control and Prevention in Atlanta for analysis.

Suzanne ran to her car and as she was preparing to leave the Administration Building's parking lot, received a message from her children's school that it was being dismissed early due to 'bus transportation issues'. As she left, she was almost creamed by another car running through a red light and driving at an alarming speed. She gasped at the mayhem on the street in front of her as cars careened madly about. It almost reminded her of a "bumper cars" carnival attraction as she witnessed two accidents in a matter of a few minutes. She had a few near misses as she drove to the University that morning, but it was nothing compared to the mayhem she now experienced. Somehow, she managed to make it to her daughters' school safely where Ana and Camila and a few other students were waiting with a teacher in the Grades 1-3 pickup area. She even had to drive around an accident in front of the school to pick them up. What was wrong with everyone? Where were the police?

She was shocked when she pulled into her driveway, and they saw a large trailer behind her husband's pickup truck. She was even more surprised when they saw four horses peeking over their back-yard fence. Ana almost fell as she stumbled over a small hay bale next to the truck on their way to the back door. When they were inside, Suzanne breathed a huge sigh of relief. What was going on, and why in hell did Tomas just buy 4 horses? While the girls ran upstairs to play, she went to find Tomas.

Chapter 4

15 YEARS LATER

The sun was setting as Ana Cordoba shoveled the last dirt onto her father Tomas' grave. She wished she had a coffin to bury him in, but the large wooden crate was the best she could find. She thought she should say something, but she couldn't think of anything, and there was no one around to hear it anyway, so she walked slowly back on a beaten path through the woods to a small ramshackle house falling apart from disrepair. This was the only house she had ever really known and now that both of her parents were gone, she knew she needed to think hard about her future.

She left the door open until she could light a candle, then closed it against a stiff wind blowing dust and mosquitos inside. She sat down at the kitchen table and stared out a small dirty window near the front door. Now what? Life had been hard for as long as she could remember, but at least she had her parents to keep her company at first until they lost their memories and she had to take care of them. Now with both parents gone, the enormity of her situation fell hard on her. She was alone in a house barely visible from the nearest road, with no neighbors around, hardly any food and no electricity or running water. She started crying until she decided she had had enough. Any other location would have to be better than this.

Early the next morning, she jumped out of her bed to take care of her father until she remembered he was gone. She slowly packed the few things she had, stuffed her father's handgun in her waistband and put on a large floppy hat. Her horse was too old to ride, so she connected a small buggy to his collar, and piled her meager belongings in the back of the buggy. As she left, the sun was starting to rise, and she knew it would be hot soon. She needed to make it to a large settlement before sundown, as it was not safe to travel at night. There were many wild and dangerous animals and the few people she sometimes met didn't seem very friendly. She suddenly felt alone and afraid as she closed the front door. She thought about locking it and laughed. She hadn't seen the key in years and anyone who wanted this house could have it. She looked back at the decrepit old house one last time and was certain that she would never come back. She could only remember being away from the house a few times in her 22 years. The last ten years had been spent taking care of her mother and father.

Her older sister Camila had left several years earlier hoping to find an easier living somewhere. She hated leaving her younger sister to care for her parents, but she hated their daily hunt for food even more and wanted to be around people other than her sister and parents that couldn't even remember who they were most of the time.

Ana didn't even know why, in the end, her parents couldn't even remember their own names or even why they should eat. Finding enough food had been a constant struggle as she was only aware of a few things that could be eaten within walking distance from the house. The only thing that had kept them alive was a small fruit and vegetable garden near the house, that her father had started when they first moved there. Unfortunately, her parents didn't know how to properly preserve and store food, so the winters were very difficult. In the last few years, she had spent most of those winter days hunting for small animals or whatever she could find near the house.

Carrying water in a bucket from the nearest freshwater stream had been difficult until she found an old buggy in a neighbor's long abandoned shed and a large vase that could hold enough water for a few days. It had taken some time to figure out how to attach the buggy to her horse's collar, so she could fill the vase from the stream and bring it back to the house.

All that was behind her now. She hoped life in a large settlement would be easier. Surely, they had some easier way to gather food and water. She had visited a large settlement a few years earlier when she needed to find some medicine for her mother's back pain. She met a guy who told her about a drugstore where she might still find something that might help her mother. She even wondered if she could find the friendly stranger who had helped her. Maybe he could help her again?

She knew her old horse needed new horseshoes, but she had never met anyone who knew how to re-shoe a horse, so she stayed off the roadway and her horse had to pull the buggy around the abandoned cars she sometimes encountered. The former interstate highway was now overgrown with bushes, grass, weeds, and small trees. Luckily, it was large enough that it was not completely covered. She was amazed at the virtual sea of wildflowers along the sides of the interstate. She started to sneeze from the wildflower pollen her horse and buggy were stirring and guided him closer to the freeway where the wildflowers were not as abundant. Just before midday she passed a faded sign that said, "Welcome to Sealy, Population 6250". Someone had painted over the 6250 and replaced it with the number 60. Ana doubted there were that many people left in the small settlement of Sealy. At least the next biggest town, Katy, should have a lot more people.

Her father had taken her to Sealy about 12 years ago to search several buildings near the old interstate for anything that might prove useful, but all of them had been completely ransacked. The only thing left were piles of empty boxes. That outing had taken all day by horse and buggy and Ana was not enthusiastic about future searches of other small towns nearby. They had rarely encountered people and when they did, her father seemed to go out of his way to avoid them.

Traveling by horse and buggy was difficult. She wished the buggy had a more comfortable seat. Her lumpy old pillow helped some, but she wasn't used to riding so long in the old buggy and it was already starting to hurt her rear. The sun was high overhead when her stomach started to growl, so she steered her horse off the highway and into a stand of trees to cool off some and to look for water for him. She found a small stream and pulled a small bucket of grain and a water bucket from the buggy and watered and fed him. She found a convenient spot and carefully used the last bit of her precious toilet paper. There was a tree stump that seemed to be free of crawling bugs and she sat down to rest and cool off. She had learned how to make a crude form of jerky and started chewing on a large piece. Fortunately, there were only a few mosquitos and flies in the small thicket of trees.

Her horse suddenly started to neigh and pulled back against the reins she had tied to a tree. She quickly pulled her handgun from her waistband, took hold of his reins, and tried to soothe him when she heard some grunting noises. In a flash, a group of small wild hogs appeared from behind some bushes and moved toward her. She quickly shot three of the hogs and the rest of the group turned and ran away. That was a lot of meat to leave behind, but she quickly threw everything back into the buggy and led her horse back to the highway. She knew that wild hogs were unpredictable, and she couldn't afford to rest any longer in case they came back in larger numbers. She didn't have many bullets left. She made a mental note to find a larger gun, or maybe even a rifle in case she came across the larger hogs. Her handgun wouldn't stop them.

Based on mile markers on the old interstate, it had taken most of the day to travel 40 miles or so and was late in the afternoon when she passed a sign that said, "Welcome to Katy, Population 22000". Someone had again painted over the old population number and written 200. She steered her horse toward the first group of houses she saw. A few random houses were lit with candles and one that looked familiar had a fireplace with smoke rising from a brick opening on the top of the house. Something smelled good and she was hungry. She tied her horse to a mailbox post in front, hesitated, then knocked on the door.

Sam Maller opened the door to a raggedly dressed young woman with long unkempt curly black hair and large dark eyes. Something tugged at his memory. He had seen her before when she came looking for some medicine for her mother.

"Hello. Ana, isn't it?"

She was surprised that he remembered her. "Yes, how did you remember me?"

"I don't have many visitors and I don't have the affliction. I'm Sam. Please come in."

She remembered him because he had helped her find medicine. He hadn't changed much. He was a little taller than her and slender with blond hair and blue eyes. He hadn't shaved in a few days and had the beginnings of a scraggly beard. He was wearing jeans and a red flannel shirt that seemed somehow to be almost new. When she walked past him carrying a large knapsack over her shoulder, he saw her horse tied to the mailbox post outside. "Did you feed your horse?"

"I would, but I don't have any more food for him."

"Make yourself comfortable. There's a bathroom just off the kitchen and some food on the table. I'll find something for your horse."

As he closed the door behind him, Ana dropped her knapsack on a chair, saw the open door of the bathroom, picked up an oil lamp in the kitchen and ran to the bathroom. She looked around for a bucket with water but there wasn't one. How did he flush the toilet? Surely the toilet didn't still flush. She slowly pressed the handle and watched with disbelief as the toilet flushed. There was even a whole roll of precious toilet paper, something else she hadn't seen in quite a while. She quickly used the toilet and found some liquid soap in a bottle by the sink. She washed her hands slowly enjoying the feel of the silky soap on her hands. This was much better than the lye soaps her mother taught her to make.

She stared at herself in a mirror over the sink. Her hair was a mess, and her face was smudged and dirty from the windy day-long trip along the former highway. She especially enjoyed washing her face with the liquid soap. It must have some moisturizers as her face and hands didn't feel as dry and rough. There were several small hand towels hanging near the sink and she used one to dry her hands. It was incredibly soft.

Sam was still outside so she started looking around and found bread and some kind of drink on a table next to the kitchen. She was hungry, but she knew she had to eat slowly, or she would be sick. The bread was still warm and quite delicious. She nibbled on it, savoring each small bite, while she looked around the kitchen. The kitchen was open to a large family room with a fireplace. The family room was lit by two oil lamps. She had grown up with some oil lamps, but they had run out of oil for them years ago. The kitchen and family room were surprisingly clean and tidier than her old country house.

She noticed a small black pot hanging over a log fire in the fireplace and carefully lifted the lid with some tongs hanging next to the fireplace. The aroma of the stew almost made her faint. She couldn't even remember the last time she had eaten warm savory meat. She forced herself to wait for Sam – she thought she should ask him if she could have some.

He returned a few minutes later and saw her waiting by the stewpot. "Help yourself."

She hungrily filled a small bowl with a ladle hanging next to the fireplace, sat down at the table and savored the aroma of the stew as she waited for it to cool a bit, so she could eat it.

He placed a water bottle near her bowl, sat at the table and drank some water. "It's been a long time since you were here. How's your mother, Suzanne I think?"

"She died a few years ago. My father died yesterday."

"I'm sorry. It must have been terrible taking care of them for so many years."

She nodded and started gobbling the stew once it cooled some. When she paused for a drink of water, she noticed he seemed lost in thought. "Are you here alone?"

"Yes, my parents died many years ago."

She returned to her stew and after a while Sam asked "So, what are you going to do now?"

"I don't know. I just know that I don't want to live so far from people anymore. Are there any empty houses in the settlement?"

He laughed. "Yes, almost all of them are empty, but no one has lived in them for years. It may not be safe for you at first. There's a lot of wildlife roaming around, and they may have taken up shelter in them."

"I know that, but I can take care of myself."

He smiled again. "Do you have a gun?"

"Yes, my father taught me to shoot when I was little - and he still knew who I was. I'm almost out of bullets, though."

Sam nodded. "You can stay here tonight and then tomorrow we can try to find you a place – and some more bullets."

"I don't have any goods to trade with you for that."

"Just having someone to talk to is payment enough."

She finished her bowl of stew and water. "Why weren't you affected by the meteor shower?"

Sam shrugged. "I don't know. A small percentage of people seemed to be immune to the meteors. I guess I was just lucky, and so were you." She nodded.

There was a cuckoo clock ticking on the wall and Ana noticed it. "Why is that thing making noise?"

"You don't know what a cuckoo clock is?"

She shook her head.

"Everyone used to have a watch or clock that told them what time of day it is."

She vaguely knew about analog clocks that kept the time, but not how to read them. All the digital clocks had stopped working when the power went out or their batteries died. "What time is it?"

"It's 7:30."

She looked out the kitchen window and shrugged. "I'll be dark soon."

"I'll explain how to read clocks with hands, sometime. In the meantime, would you like to take a bath and clean up some? The last time you were here, you said you lived west of Sealy and that's about 20 miles from here. You must have been travelling all day in your buggy."

"Oh, yes, please."

"Follow me." He picked up two oil lamps and handed her one and she slung her knapsack over her shoulder and followed him up a flight of stairs, down a hallway and into a bathroom. She was thinking he meant a bucket and sponge bath, but this bathroom had an actual bathtub. She hadn't taken a bath in a bathtub since she was little and when there was plenty of water.

He gestured toward the tub. "There you go. The toilet in here flushes as well."

"A bath like that would waste a lot of water."

"I have plenty." He turned on the bathtub faucets and she was shocked to see water flowing into the tub. She could even see wisps of steam rising from the tub – that meant hot water!

"You have hot water?"

"Yes, I have a solar-powered pump that fills two cisterns on the roof and a solar water heater that heats one of the tanks during the day."

"Is the water safe to drink?"

"Yes, there is a hardware store near here that still has a large supply of water treatment chemicals and test kits, mostly to keep swimming pools safe, but I use them to keep the water in the cistern tanks clean and safe to drink, or shower or even flush the toilets."

She didn't understand all that. She only knew that she wanted to take a hot bath. She seemed to be waiting for him to leave, so he closed the door behind him. She quickly undressed, used the toilet, and stepped into the warm water. She even found a bar of soap that smelled wonderful and a shampoo bottle on a niche above the tub and enjoyed her first hot bath in many years. There were several large towels hanging near the tub and she was surprised they seemed even softer than the small hand towel. The lye soaps her mother had shown her how to make to wash their clothes and towels made them rather rough and stiff. Not at all like these towels.

She pulled the plug from the tub and wondered where all that water was going. She knew the sewer systems had not worked for many years.

Several tubes of toothpaste were stacked in a cabinet over the sink. She pulled her old toothbrush out of her bag and carefully squeezed some toothpaste on it. The taste was wonderful compared to the baking soda she had used for years.

Sam was sitting by the fire reading a book when she came down the stairs with a different outfit on. He noticed her dark curly hair was still damp. She sat down in another chair by the fireplace.

"That bath was wonderful. We didn't have enough water to do that." Her old house had a bathroom, but water had stopped flowing years ago, so her father built an outhouse in the back yard. She really didn't understand how Sam managed to keep everything working. "My dad once said the sewers don't work anymore, where did the bathwater go?"

"When this house was built, the street was pretty far from town and all the houses had septic tanks. As the city grew, eventually this neighborhood was connected to the city's sewer system. Years ago, when the power and water treatment systems went down, I re-connected the house sewer line to the septic tank."

She frowned. "What's a septic tank?"

"It's an underground tank that allows wastewater solids to settle on the bottom. When there's enough water it flows out near the top through some filters into the ground. Eventually you have to pump out the solids and dispose of them. But it can take years before you have to do that when only one person is using it. The septic tank for this house is really big as they are sized by the number of bedrooms in the house."

Ana was still trying to understand that as he continued. "This was a really nice house at one time. It has five bedrooms and three baths. It's probably not safe to wander around outside now, so you are welcome to stay in any bedroom upstairs."

"Thanks for helping me."

"Glad I could."

"By the way, how do you clean the towels and washcloths?" They feel so nice."

Sam laughed. "Like they used to do before there was electricity – with a tub and washboard. I hang them to dry out back."

"I haven't felt anything that soft in many years."

"I use a softener in the rinse water."

She seemed puzzled. "Softener?"

"I'm not sure how it works, but my mom used to use it all the time, so I do. It seems to make a difference."

"The towels are really soft and smell really nice."

Sam smiled as he wondered how she used to do it. He started to ask her when she yawned and thanked him again and carried her knapsack up the stairs with an oil lamp to guide her and found a bedroom with a large bed. She hadn't slept on anything that comfortable in many years. The mattress in her old bed had holes and broken springs and she had found a way to sleep on it, so the springs didn't hurt her. This bed was very soft, and she fell asleep almost as soon as she undressed, put on one of her mother's old nightgowns and laid down.

Chapter 5

A NEW START

The next morning the sun was already up when she woke. She jumped out of bed and suddenly realized she didn't need to take care of her father anymore and she was in a different house. She dressed and, as quietly as she could, carried her knapsack down the stairs to the kitchen in case he was still asleep. Sam was reading a repair manual at the table and something that smelled like sweet bread was sitting on the table. He looked up.

"Did you sleep okay?"

"Oh, yes! That bed was very soft."

"Are you hungry? I made some sweet rolls."

She nodded and sat down quickly and started eating one of the sweet rolls. She stared at the sugar coating on the roll.

"How do you still have bread…and sugar?"

"This house has a dry and well-insulated basement. Right after the power went out, I stored a lot of stuff like flour and sugar in there in multiple layers of sealable plastic bags. I still have quite a bit left. I built a log oven out back to bake the bread."

"I haven't had anything with sugar in many years."

"Do you like coffee?"

"I've heard about it, but I don't remember ever drinking any. What does it taste like?"

He shrugged. "I don't know, like coffee…" He placed a cup of dark liquid on the table in front of her. It smelled like roasted nuts. She sipped on it slowly as it was hot.

"This is good. How do you know so much about the time before the meteors?"

"I was eighteen when it happened, and I haven't forgotten anything."

She thought about that as she finished the roll and the coffee. She would like to know more about the time before the meteors, but there were more important things to take care of first.

"You said you could help me find a place today?"

"Yes, but what do you plan to do? It's not very likely that anyone else will help you very much. Most people are too busy staying alive to help other people. Do you have any skills, or can you make things you can exchange for other stuff you need?"

"I don't know, maybe. I guess I could take care of people that are losing their memories. I have a lot of experience doing that."

Sam laughed. "You may be able to find a few people like that. Anything else?"

"I like to paint pictures, but I don't think anyone would trade anything of value for my paintings."

"Okay. So that's something we can work on. In the meantime, do you know how to play checkers or chess? I haven't been able to play table games in years."

"I know how to play checkers and chess, but I'm not very good."

"That doesn't matter. Just having to something to take your mind off things every now and then, helps a lot." He thought for a moment. "Can you play any musical instruments?"

"I can play the guitar, but my guitar had so many broken strings, I left it behind."

"Can you read music?"

"We didn't have any sheet music and I couldn't find any when we went looking for supplies from time to time. So, I play by ear." She paused. "You once showed me a drugstore and mentioned a food store. Does that still have food?"

"Yes, most of the food went bad when the power went out, but there is still some food in cans and glass jars that might be okay to eat. But you never know what you'll find when you open a can or glass jar that's years beyond its expiration date."

"That's okay, it's all I need to get started."

Sam finished his coffee. "All right. Let's go see if we can find a place you like."

She watched him put on a hat and a holster with a handgun. He tossed some plastic packages of jerky into a backpack with several water bottles then slipped his arms into the backpack, picked up a rifle from a rack on the wall and opened the door for her.

She emptied her knapsack onto a chair and put on her large floppy hat and her gun in the waistband of her pants, slung the knapsack over her shoulder and walked out the door to find some food and possibly a new home.

The settlement had once been a town of about 22,000 but now held only about a hundred residents and a lot of wildlife, including deer, raccoons, wild hogs, possums, dogs, and occasional coyotes.

As they began walking along the street in front of Sam's house, Ana heard some growling noises and saw Sam shift his rifle to a ready position. A few seconds later a pack of wild dogs sprang from some large bushes near the road and charged at them. Sam shot the nearest dog and was surprised when Ana quickly shot two more. The rest of the pack fled back to the safety of the bushes.

"You're pretty good with a handgun."

"I used to hunt squirrels and nutria. You sort of have to sneak up on them. If you miss you don't eat. I killed a small hog once, but it was a lot of work to clean it, and I didn't like the taste of the meat."

He agreed. "I don't like hog meat either. They used to make sausage out of the meat that was pretty good, but I don't know how to make it and haven't had any in years." He examined the nearest dog. "I don't eat dogs, but these are rabid anyway." He pulled some rubber gloves out of his backpack and dragged the dead dogs off the road. "The hogs and the vultures can have these."

As they walked along the street, Ana tried to imagine what the houses looked like when the yards were mowed, and the bushes and trees were trimmed. She could barely see some houses now as the grass, bushes and weeds were taller than her. They didn't have to go very far until they found a large house that seemed to be in pretty good shape.

"How about this one?"

"It seems like a huge house. Why this one?"

"A friend of mine's family used to live there. It was a nice house."

It didn't appear to be occupied, and as they approached the house, Sam saw a small window that was slightly open, pushed it open, and crawled inside. He soon opened the front door for her, and she entered the large house and looked around in amazement.

Although it was extremely dusty with cobwebs everywhere, the beauty of the home was evident. There was a massive wooden staircase and stone floors and several stained-glass windows. She pulled the gun from her waistband and walked quickly through the house looking for animals or anything that could be a danger if she stayed there. Sam followed her pointing out some of the house's features.

"It looks okay. All the doors and windows are still intact. There's no sign of rodents or hogs or snakes or dogs or anything that might harm you."

This house was even bigger than Sam's house. "It's probably too big for me."

"Why not try it out? You can find something else if it's not right."

"How did you choose the house you live in?"

"It was my parent's house. I grew up there. It was easy for me to fortify it over time and keep as many systems working as I could."

"How do you know so much about how things work?"

"I was going to be an auto mechanic and took a lot of trade type classes in high school. I was studying in a vocational school when the meteor shower happened. That training helped me a lot. The hardware store near my house that has everything I could ever need to fix stuff."

"I don't know much about fixing things."

Sam rubbed his beard stubble. "Do you know how to cook?"

"I can cook but we didn't have much food. I did the best I could."

"Maybe we could get together from time to time, and you could fix some meals and I could help you fix things in the house."

She nodded. "That sounds fair."

She followed Sam as he walked about the house checking everything to see what condition it was in. He finally stopped, pulled out a conductor's watch and glanced at it. "It's almost 10 AM. Maybe we should go to the food store and find some stuff for you. I have a pantry full of stuff."

They walked out the front door and Sam started searching the bushes, flowerpots and other items near the front door.

"What are you doing?"

"Sometimes people kept a spare door key somewhere near the front door in case they locked themselves out." He continued searching until he found it under a flowerpot. He stood upright. "Found it!"

She watched him lock the front door. He handed her the key and she stared at it. "Why do you need to lock the door?"

"The few people who weren't affected by the meteors includes a few bad people who will hurt you if they can, just for fun or because they have mental problems."

Ana just shook her head and started following Sam to the food store. As they were walking, he asked "would you like some new clothes?"

"Oh, yes! These were my mom's clothes. Is there a clothing store that might have something that would fit me?"

"There are several clothing stores near here that still have some usable clothes in plastic bags inside boxes. The stuff that was displayed on shelves or hanging on racks or on mannequins isn't usable. We'll stop there first."

He pulled several small jerky packages and water bottles from his backpack and handed some to her. She stared at a plastic jerky package for a moment then opened it. The spicy smell made her even hungrier, and they started munching on the jerky as they headed for the clothing store. This was a lot better than the crude jerky she had learned to make. "How do you know when jerky is still okay to eat?"

"First, look at the color, then see if there's any mold growing in it. Don't bother to open it unless it looks okay. Then smell it. It should have a strong spice smell. If it's rancid, or just doesn't smell right, don't eat it. I keep a cache of beef jerky in the basement of my house where it's kept cool all the time. That seems to make a difference."

"How about the food left in the store."

"I'll show you. But let's find some new clothes for you first."

Chapter 6

SHOPPING OUTING

Sam led Ana to a large strip shopping center. Ana had never seen so many kinds of stores before. This was a lot larger than the small shopping area in Sealy that wasn't too far from her home, but those stores had been vandalized and stripped of all their merchandise and she had only visited it once with her father.

This shopping center was different. She passed a few stores with the windows still intact that still contained some merchandise. Most of the windows of the clothing store were very dirty but intact. Several sheets of plywood covered a few windows and the door had combination lock on it.

"Some friends helped me with this. We wanted to keep the birds and wild animals out."

He opened the combination lock and held the door open. Ana entered the dark store filled with dusty mannequins and tattered clothing piled on shelves. Most of the clothes on display were damaged from insects, cockroaches, moths, silverfish, and spiders. He led her to the storeroom in back and pulled a flashlight out of his backpack. Ana watched him crank a handle and in a few seconds his beam lit the dusty shelves. She followed him as he walked along the storeroom aisles. He stopped and handed her several boxes.

"You might be a six or eight. I don't know that much about women's clothes."

Ana opened one of the boxes and stared at the plastic bag with a pair of jeans that looked to be in perfect condition. She started to take off her pants to try them on.

Sam laughed. "I think you might want to do that in a fitting room."

Ana stared at him with a blank expression.

He took another hand-crank flashlight out of his backpack and handed it to her. "Let me show you".

She followed his example, cranked the handle, and followed him back into the back of the store.

His flashlight illuminated a fitting room sign. "In there."

In the fitting room, she set her flashlight on a shelf and tried on several pairs of jeans, but the size 6 jeans were an almost perfect fit. She found him waiting near the stockroom door holding a small stack of boxes. He stared at her for a moment. He didn't know she had such a slim body. He held out the boxes. "I think these might fit you as well."

She opened the boxes and found several more pairs of jeans, some underwear, and a few frilly blouses, and laughed. "These don't look like they would last very long."

"That's okay. They don't have to. You can have as many as you need or want."

She nodded and returned to the fitting room to try some on. A few minutes later, Sam had to stare again. Free at last from her mother's ill-fitting and oversized clothes, Ana's hourglass figure was striking. Sam smiled.

"Wow! You look great! You might want to put on a bra though."

"I've never worn one."

"Just a minute." He walked to the storeroom and returned with a stack of small boxes. "One of these may fit."

Ana opened the top box and took out a brassiere. "This doesn't look comfortable."

"It probably isn't but after a while you'll see why women wore them all the time."

She shrugged and returned to the fitting room. When she came out, Sam nodded. "That's perfect."

"Perfectly awful, but I'll try it for a while. I would like to have a few more shirts, though. I don't want to wear the same thing every day if there are choices."

"Like I do, you mean."

She laughed. "You can have as many shirts and jeans as you want – too."

When she turned to look for more clothes, Sam noticed the size on the empty brassiere box was a 38C and muttered "whoa".

As soon as Ana added a few more items to her knapsack and Sam added a few jeans to his, he locked the clothing store's front door and they left for the food store.

"How come there's so much clothing left? All the stores in Sealy were completely stripped of everything. The only thing left were boxes."

"I don't know. Every town was affected differently by the meteors. When the food shortages started, some people left their towns and cities to look for food. By the time the power went out in Katy, almost everyone had either lost their memory or left the town. I guess there weren't that many people left to take everything from the stores."

They hadn't seen anyone all day and Ana remembered the population signs. "I passed a population sign on the old freeway that someone had changed to 220 people. Are there that many people still here?"

"No, people are still losing their memories and not leaving their houses, or they are still leaving the town hoping to find food somewhere."

"That's why I left Sealy..."

Food Store

The food store was a short walk from the clothing store in the same strip shopping center. The food store windows were also extremely dirty but largely intact. Ana could see the same simple repairs and lock on the door as the clothing store. Sam opened the combination lock and held the door open for her. They pulled out their flashlights, cranked them and entered the dark store.

There was a strong musty odor combined with a cloud of dust as they walked around the store. Ana coughed a few times.

Most of the shelves were empty, but some still held some cans, jars and boxes.

"We threw out all the rotten food years ago. It was pretty gross, and it took some time to kill all the bugs and rodents that were feasting on the rotting food. There's still some food here that's in cans and glass jars that might be okay. Just don't take any can that's all puffed up, or a glass jar with a puffed-up lid. That's bad for sure."

"What about the food in boxes?"

"That's probably not good, but you have to open it and look for bugs and mold to be sure. If there's a plastic bag inside the box, it may still be okay to eat."

Ana noticed a row of shopping carts near the windows by the front door. "Can we take one of those to carry stuff back?"

"Something or someone broke some of the front windows years ago, and with the wind blowing rain on them, most of them are now rusted and stuck together. It's probably not worth the effort to pry them apart and find one that still rolls easily."

Ana cranked the flashlight handle again and went off to look for food on the mostly empty aisles containing a few cans and glass jars. A few minutes later she came back straining to carry her backpack obviously loaded with cans and jars.

"Here, let's swap backpacks. That looks pretty heavy."

Ana traded backpacks. "Thanks that would be pretty heavy to carry back. How did you bring so many cans and jars back to your house?"

"I found a small cart in the hardware store. I managed to get it rolling again and use that once a month to carry a lot of stuff back."

He motioned her to follow him. "Let's see if any of this is edible." There was a small deli area in the front of the store with a few tables and chairs. He put her backpack on one of the tables and pulled out a few cans, examining them.

"These seem okay, but let's open one to be sure." He pulled a small can opener from a pocket in his jeans and showed it to her. "Never leave home without one of these."

She watched him open a can of sliced peaches. He handed it to her. "If it looks okay, see how it smells."

Ana had never eaten peaches before, but she didn't see any mold and the aroma from the can reminded her of some wildflowers. "It seems okay."

She handed it back to him. He pulled a pocketknife from another pocket and pulled out a slice of peach and carefully bit off a piece. "I think it's okay. Try it." He handed her his knife.

Ana tried her first peach. It had a nice texture and was very sweet. "It's good."

Sam pulled out a can of diced tomatoes and noticed it had a dent on the side. "Cans with dents can be bad. Some manufacturers put a special coating on the inside of the can to prevent foods from rusting. Dents can cause rust and sometimes bacteria to grow."

He checked the can thoroughly. "The top, bottom and side seams look okay, but let's open it see." He opened the can and they both held their noses. "That's not good."

Sam watched Ana pulled all the cans and jars out of her backpack examining them carefully. She discarded two that seemed bloated, or the seams didn't seem quite right. He watched her starting to put the remaining cans back in the backpack.

"Don't worry about throwing out the questionable cans and jars, we can always find some more."

Sam's backpack also contained some cans and jars that he had already checked. He looked at his pocket watch. "We better start back. We don't want to be out when the sun starts to go down."

"Why not?"

"In addition to the wildlife looking for food, that's when the crazy and mean people come out to cause trouble."

Sam locked the grocery store's door, and they headed back to her new house.

"There isn't a lot of food left in the store. What will you do when it's all gone?"

"One of my friend's dad is a farmer or was a commercial farmer until there was no more fuel for the tractors and trucks. I helped him make a plow that could be pulled by horses. He has a few old horses left and now farms a few acres each year. I sometimes trade my labor fixing things in his house for some fresh food."

"I wish I had something I could trade for food when the store is empty."

"You'll have a while to figure that out."

Chapter 7

FIRST EVENING

It was still early evening when they arrived back at Ana's new home. She unlocked the door, and they carried the knapsacks of food to the kitchen. "Can you make the water work here too?"

"Maybe. It depends on how bad the plumbing is. I have a spare solar-powered water pump and hose and there's a freshwater stream that isn't too far from here. Finding storage tanks to hold water might be difficult."

She placed a few candles on the kitchen counter and lit them with some matches from the store. "See, that's better."

Sam just smiled as he pulled his handgun out of his holster. "I need to be going before it gets dark. Keep the doors locked and don't have any candles on that can be seen from the street."

"Okay." She walked over and hugged him. "Thanks for helping me."

"I'm happy to have someone to talk to. I'll bring the rest of your stuff by tomorrow. Okay, see you then."

She locked the door behind him and started fixing a few things to eat. She opened several cans of vegetables before she found two that were still good. She had found a few cans of Sterno and a box of kitchen matches in the grocery store and used those to warm the canned vegetables. There were some strange noises outside and she put most of the candles out, making sure the ones still lit could not be seen from the street.

After she finished eating, she heard some more noises in the street and put the remaining candles out and peeked out behind a front window's curtain. There was a small group of people carrying torches and walking in the street. Some others were walking from house to house checking the front doors to see if they were open. Ana confirmed the front door was locked, ran to her knapsack in the kitchen and found her gun. She needed a better place to defend herself if it came to that. She headed up the stairs and found a place she could watch the front door. Someone rattled the front door and moved on with the crowd in the street. She breathed a sigh of relief. She quickly searched the upstairs area to make sure the stairs were the only way up and was relieved that there was no other way.

She pulled an old dusty pillow and moth-ridden blanket off a bed and laid down at the top of the stairs. She didn't want to be surprised in case they returned.

Early the next morning, she sat on the stairs thinking about the house. There was no water, no heat and really no reason to stay there. The downstairs floors were stone and cold on her feet. The house was probably well insulated as it seemed cool inside even when it was warm outside. It would probably be pretty cold in the winter with no heat. Maybe she could stay with Sam for a while until she really figured out if she wanted to stay in the settlement or move on. His house had water and a fireplace and comfortable beds. She put the remaining groceries back in her knapsack and locked the front door. She was pretty sure she could find his house....

The tall weeds and grass made it hard to find his house and she walked down several wrong streets. It took most of the morning, but she finally found Sam's house. She suddenly remembered her horse! She hoped he was okay. She found him in the back of the house in a small structure eating some grain from a bucket and found another bucket she filled with water for him.

She knocked on the door, but Sam didn't answer. She wondered if he were out for a while and sat down on the front porch to wait for him.

Later, Sam returned wearing a large backpack and found Ana waiting for him on his porch. Her large knapsack was next to her.

"Is there something wrong with the house?"

"No, it's just too much for me. There's no water or heat and I just don't need something that big. I was wondering if I could stay with you for a while, until I figure out what I want to do."

"Sure." He unlocked the door and followed her in.

"Thanks for feeding my horse. I haven't really been away from home in a long time, so I sort of forgot about him."

"That's okay. Are you hungry? I have lots of stew."

She thought about that. Her stomach reminded her she hadn't eaten anything that morning. "Yes, that would be great." She ran to the bathroom and when she returned, she watched him light a fire in the fireplace and hang the stewpot over the fire. "I thought you said you didn't know how to cook. That stew is really good."

He laughed. "I can't do much in the cooking area, but I can open cans." He walked to the pantry and opened the door. It was packed with all sorts of cans including a stack of beef stew cans. She laughed.

"I have a lot of seasonings and spices that might still be good. I hoped to learn to cook someday, but there always seemed to be a lot to do that was more important."

She stood next to him examining the spices. "I don't know what all these are, but it might be fun to learn."

"I have a cookbook."

She had a confused expression until he commented "that's a book that tells you how to make things taste good with spices."

"I can read some, but you might have to help me with some of the words."

"We can worry about that later."

Chapter 8

A COMFORTABLE ROUTINE

They often took daily outings to several stores in the former mall near the city but were careful to be home well before dark. Ana found several more outfits that fit her slender body and she even found some different clothes for Sam. He usually just wore jeans and a shirt as it seemed he was always fixing something around the house. He tried to explain what he was doing and why he was doing it to her, but it took a while before it all made sense. She even became somewhat handy with tools.

Each night after dinner, they would snuggle and talk on the sofa about the day's events and even the future. Even though a week had passed, there had been no relationship type conversations, Sam knew the present situation could not remain the same forever. For his part, he had been immediately attracted to Ana, but he could not tell from their time together and conversations if she felt the same. One night, he decided to find out and point-blank asked her if she wanted more than a roommate.

"What do you mean?"

"Normally, there's a lot more to living together than sharing household duties. I would have also said sharing expenses but there really aren't any expenses."

Ana stared at him with a confused expression, so he felt he had to ask.

"Would you be okay with more than friendship?"

Ana smiled. "Yes. But I don't know exactly what you want as I've never had a boyfriend before."

"So, you've never done it?"

She laughed. "That would have been pretty unlikely with no guys around when I was growing up, wouldn't it?" She realized what he was asking. "Do you want to?"

"Oh, yes!" He leaned over and kissed her. She kissed him back and eventually they were lying on the sofa exploring each other with their hands, until she whispered into his ear.

"What about birth control?"

He let out a sigh at the loss of momentum and sat up. "All the birth control bills left in drugstores have long expired. And for some reason, all the condoms disappeared a long time ago."

"How do you know that?"

"I had a girlfriend a few years ago and she asked the same thing, so I looked."

Ana sat up, seemingly concerned at this revelation. "What happened to her?"

"She broke it off." Sam went on to explain. "She was my neighbor's daughter."

"The farmer?"

"Yes, I guess she wanted something more, because she left with some of her girlfriends to live somewhere in North Houston." He saw the concerned expression on her face. "No, I haven't seen her since she left."

Ana wondered what else she didn't know about Sam. "So, what do we do?"

"Well, we could try rhythm. I know that's not very reliable, but…"

Ana sat thinking. She had her last period right before she left Sealy. She started counting the days. "It's been a little more than two weeks since my last period."

Sam shook his head. "Don't ask me about a woman's period…"

Ana smiled, "Tonight. Then we should wait until it's not an issue."

Sam was suddenly energized. She laughed when he picked her up and carried her into the bedroom.

Life with Sam became routine. He usually found some time during each day to help her read the cookbook. She was a fast learner and soon they were eating dinners that were much better than the cans in the pantry. They started playing checkers and chess at night and Sam was amazed at how quickly she improved her game. She was soon beating him regularly at chess.

Although they were careful to avoid contaminated food, both became ill after opening a label-less can of "mystery" meat that smelled okay and looked okay but tasted "odd". The next morning Ana threw up and Sam spent the morning in the bathroom. Seeing Ana sick was a wake-up call for Sam that they needed to be extremely careful when they resumed having sex.

Even though life with Sam was far better than her former existence in the remote house, just the thought of having a child with no medical assistance scared Ana.

What Really Happened

A few weeks passed and one evening as they were snuggling on the sofa, Ana asked Sam what happened 15 years ago. Her parents couldn't tell her very much by the time she was old enough to understand.

"I don't know exactly what happened, but about 15 years ago there was a big meteor shower one night. It was really spectacular, but something about it was wrong."

"Wrong?"

"Yes. The next few days, there were TV reports with scientists from NASA and the equivalent scientific organizations in Europe. They had analyzed the shower and said it was mathematically impossible but the flyby paths of the all the meteors had completely covered the Earth. A few days later someone found pieces of one of the meteors and when they were analyzed, the scientists found it was not a natural meteor but manufactured and not of Earth origin. They also found a chemical on one of the pieces and it took almost a year, but they finally identified the chemical structure of the powder. When the powder was inhaled, it slowly produced symptoms like dementia or Alzheimer's. You basically lose all your memories until you can no longer remember anything – even the need to eat – and eventually even the need to breathe."

Ana was staring off into space, until she said. "Not everyone was affected. You weren't!"

"That's right, and it appears that you weren't either. Everyone was affected differently. Some started losing their memories right away, while others took many years – probably like your parents. A very small percentage, like us, were not affected at all. There was a crash program to find a cure but the scientists studying it lost their memories before a cure was found."

"Soon after the meteor shower, some people started forgetting how to drive. There were a lot of auto accidents, and it became dangerous just to drive anywhere. The police were helpless to stop it as there were so many accidents. Once the truckers couldn't deliver anything there were food shortages and bad people started breaking into people's homes to steal whatever food they could find."

Ana sat thinking. "Meteor…" She stood up, opened her backpack, and took out a shiny triangular metal piece. "My mother gave me this. She said something about the meteor shower."

She started to hand it to Sam, but he jumped off the sofa and backed up to the kitchen door. "Holy shit! "

"What's wrong?"

"The chemical on that thing can wipe out whatever memories we have left."

"No, my mother said this has been totally cleaned. There isn't any chemical in it."

Sam slowly walked back to her, and she handed it to him. This piece was several inches on each side and resembled a sponge with numerous small holes on each side. It was extremely light.

"Where did your mother get this?"

"She only said she found it." She sat back down on the sofa and Sam sat down next to her still examining the meteor fragment. One of the oil lamps in the kitchen went out and it reminded her of when they lost power.

"We had power when I was little, then it went out."

"Yes, it took almost 5 years but eventually there weren't enough workers left at the power companies that knew how to keep everything running – how to keep the power on. All the refineries and water treatment plants also went off-line around the same time. Basically, we went back to the 19th century – before there was power and running water. My father bought several horses just before the power went out. He said it was just a matter of time before all the gasoline and diesel was gone and we would be back to riding in buggies and on horses. There was a lot of trouble when the power went out – rioting, looting and so on. It was ugly."

"That's probably why my mother and father moved to the country – to be away from people and trouble. My father bought some horses right after the meteor shower and people started driving crazily."

Sam nodded. "That was smart and probably why you are still alive. Your horse must be very old by now."

"Yes, he is the last of the horses my father bought. I think he doesn't have many years left." She sat thinking. "Have you driven a car?"

"Yes, I still have a car in the garage that my parents bought for me when I was 16. It was a lot of fun until there was no more gasoline."

"Why did all this happen? Did they ever figure that out?"

"No. They just assumed that some intelligent species figured out a way to get rid of most of us for some reason, without destroying everything like a war would."

"It's been fifteen years since the meteor shower. Maybe they forgot about us?"

"Not likely. They may be waiting until the effects of the chemical are gone."

They sat there thinking until Ana stood up and held out her hand. Sam looked at her with a huge question mark.

"My period's over…" Sam jumped up and kissed her several times. She took his hand and led him into the bedroom.

Chapter 9

NEIGHBOR

The next day, there was a knock on the door. Sam answered it and seemed pleasantly surprised.

"John, how are you? I haven't seen you in a while." Sam motioned him to come in.

"I'm fine, I just need your help fixing a few things. By the way, Susan said to say hi."

Ana walked in from the kitchen and heard the comment.

"John, this is Ana Cordoba, my girlfriend." He looked at Ana. "This is John Tenney."

John seemed surprised at the girlfriend comment but shook her hand. He guessed that Ana was about the same age as his daughter, Susan.

Sam turned to Ana. "John is the farmer I mentioned. He grows a few acres and I help him fix things in exchange for some of his produce."

Ana nodded. Sam and John started discussing some repairs needed on his farm and Ana returned to the kitchen, but she could still hear their conversation.

When the "business" side of the discussion ended, John asked about Ana.

"How long have you two been together?"

"Not too long, several months."

"I had always hoped you and Susan would get back together."

Sam shook his head. "I don't think so. She broke up with me, remember? Have you heard from her lately?"

"She came by a week or so ago with her girlfriends and stayed a few days, just to catch up and let me know she's okay. They left early in the morning as they said it's not safe to travel in the evening or especially after sunset. I miss her, but I know it's not easy to stay in touch when you have to travel by horse or buggy just to talk to someone."

Sam nodded. "I know, I don't even see my neighbors much anymore, except for you."

John nodded and eventually when he left, Ana found Sam and asked about Susan.

"Who's Susan?"

"John's daughter. The former girlfriend I mentioned. It looks like her dad hardly hears from her anymore. It's hard when you have to travel by horse or buggy to stay in touch."

Ana heard what he said but immediately started thinking about Sam and Susan, probably in his house, in the kitchen, in the bed.

"I know what you're thinking but she broke up with me, and I wouldn't trade ten of her for you."

Ana was still wrestling with the idea of Sam and Susan, but she hugged him.

Sam decided to change the subject. "By the way, I asked John if he would take your horse and put it out to pasture with his other horses and he said he would. I told him I would ask you about it first."

Ana thought about it for a while, but eventually decided she would never need a horse again. She would miss him, of course, but knew that he would be better off in a pasture with other horses to keep him company.

She told Sam to take her horse to John the next time he went to the farm to fix things.

Chapter 10

RESISTANCE

Just like any other afternoon, Ana and Sam were returning from the shopping center carrying a few clothing bags. Six men wearing camouflage clothing and carrying shotguns, handguns and rifles stepped from behind trees and bushes and confronted them. Their first thought was this could be a potential robbery. Sam and Ana both had handguns, but the armed men were all pointing their shotguns and rifles at them, so he put his arm around Ana and pulled her closer. "What do you want?"

The apparent leader was older than the rest. He had a dark complexion with dark hair and eyes. Sam guessed he was in his early 40s. He was a little taller than Sam and was wearing hunting camouflage. He stared at Ana for a moment, then asked "Is your name Sam Maller?"

"Yes?"

"We need your help."

"What do you need my help for?"

"We've heard that you know a lot about how to fix things."

"Who told you that?"

"It doesn't matter. We need your help, to fight the aliens."

"Aliens?"

"You don't know?"

"Know what?"

"Earth was invaded by aliens from outer space six months ago."

Ana and Sam looked at each other. Sam was skeptical. "I didn't see or hear anything."

"Well maybe not, but they're here."

"Where?"

"The nearest group landed near Houston and has set up a type of encampment."

Sam shook his head in disbelief. "Even if that's true, why do you need my help?"

"We hope you can help us establish communication with other humans who want to fight the aliens. We don't know how to do it."

"I just know how to fix things. Not create new ways to communicate."

"We know about things like telegraphs. Maybe you could help get them to work."

"We're probably okay in this small town, so I'm not interested."

The leader pointed his handgun at Sam. "Our beef is with the aliens, not with you, but we will keep your woman with us until you agree."

Ana tightened her grip on Sam's arm.

"How long would I have to be away from her?"

"Not too long – as soon as we can communicate with others like us, you can go back to her."

Ana and Sam looked at each other. "I won't be away one minute longer than I need to be."

"I know. Just be careful."

He kissed her, and she watched him walk off with the resistance fighters. As soon as they were out of sight, she hurried back home.

Chapter 11

TELEGRAPH

The resistance fighters led Sam to a large warehouse. It was full of items gathered by the resistance fighters including weapons, beds and piles of electronics. Instead of oil lamps or candles, the warehouse was lit by a dozen torches attached to the walls. It almost seemed to be something out of a bad dream. Sam counted about twenty men and a dozen or so women in the warehouse. Some were cleaning weapons, others eating. Most looked extremely bored.

The leader offered Sam a water bottle. "My name is Arun Patel. I'm sort of in charge here because I was in the army reserves for years and no one else has any kind of military training. A few years ago, some of us formed an ad hoc neighborhood watch group as a protection against the roving gangs of thugs that prey on defenseless people. When we found out about the aliens, we held a vote and formed this group to fight the aliens. There probably aren't many humans left, but we can't let them take over without a fight."

Sam listened carefully as he drank some water. "What do you want me to do?"

"We found some old telegraph machines in a railroad museum. We were hoping to be able to use it to communicate to others who want to fight the aliens." He laughed. "Pigeons are a terrible way to communicate by the way. We tried. And all other forms of communication require some form of power, which we don't have."

"If we can come up with a power source, wouldn't a shortwave or HAM radio be easier to use? Telegraphs will require using old telephone or power lines to carry the signal. You may never get that to work."

"We thought about wireless type communications, but the aliens would probably be able to intercept them and track those signals right to us."

Sam thought about that while Ted led him to a pair of old telegraph machines connected to several large batteries. "We don't have any power to charge the batteries."

"What about solar cells?"

"We found some, but they are pretty old now and we aren't sure how to hook them up."

"Even if we got these machines working somehow, who are you going to talk to?"

"There are others like us. Right now, we travel by horse to try and discuss common strategies. There is a group like us in Baytown but it's more than 50 miles east of here and it takes all day to travel there by horse. Someone in that group told us they heard there were more alien encampments near Dallas and San Antonio. If that's true, there may be dozens of encampments in North America alone. Having a telegraph to communicate quickly would be immensely helpful. We did some preliminary checking, and we think we can probably use some old phone lines not too far from here for the telegraph wire. We brought several rolls of wire from a hardware store to test the machines."

Sam examined the telegraph units. They were old and dusty but seemed to be intact. He needed to find a way to charge their batteries. A quick inspection of the batteries confirmed their electrodes were too corroded to re-charge.

"These old gravity cells are actually a variant of the Daniell cells first used in telegraphs and can't be charged."

"Why not?"

"The zinc electrodes are corroded and almost eaten away from sitting in a concentrated acid solution for years without being used – charged and discharged. But I may have a solution."

"What is it?"

"Most small batteries, whether lead and acid, or nickel alloy or lithium typically only have a five to ten-year storage life - max. A few new lithium batteries supposedly had a twenty-year life, but they were only around for a few years before the power went out and there was no way to prove that was true or not. Until we could find some of those, we need to find some car batteries that were shipped to a retail auto parts outlet without the acid solution, then find and add the acid and charge them slowly."

"Where can we find some batteries like that?"

Sam shrugged. "I have a few. I found them years ago in an old tire and battery store in Houston, but they are probably near the end of their life by now."

"Can you find that store again?"

"I don't know. I found it a few years ago, but I have a general idea where it is."

"We can look tomorrow. For now, let's find some food for you."

He led Sam to a corner of the warehouse where two tables had been set up buffet style. Some of the food smelled delicious. He turned to Arun. "Where did you get all this? None of the food stores I've been to have any prepared foods that are still edible."

Arun pointed to one of the resistance members. "He used to live next door to a doomsday prepper. When he joined us, he told us about his neighbor and we found an underground bunker in the guy's back-yard that was full of survival food, enough to last us years if we are careful with it."

The food that Ana had learned to prepare with some spices had been delicious (compared to eating out of cans) but this was on a much higher level. And the only thing they needed to do in most cases was add water to the packages and heat them over a campfire. Sam wished Ana could be there to enjoy the spread laid out before him.

Sam picked up his water bottle and it triggered something in the back of his mind. "Where are you getting your drinking water and the water for the food?"

Arun guessed why he was asking. "We found a huge stash of water bottles in a warehouse not too far from here. Don't worry, it's safe."

While they were eating, Arun asked "where did you meet your woman?"

"Her name is Ana. Why do you ask?"

"She sure looks a lot like someone I met somewhere. I just can't remember where."

"A few years ago, she came to Katy looking for some medicine to help her mother. When her mother and father died, she came back looking for a new place to live. She said she was tired of living in the middle of nowhere and wanted to be near people."

That reply triggered a memory in Arun. "Oh yeah! One of our guys has a brother who has a girlfriend that looks like Ana, and I heard her make the same comment once."

"Ana said she had a sister who left home a few years ago. I wonder if that's her."

"We may find out in a few days. We ask them to find things we need and when they do, they trade them to us for food. Lucky for us, they haven't found some prepper's food stash yet."

Sam wondered if Ana had ever contacted her sister since she left home. She didn't talk much about her.

Telegraph Batteries

It took most of the day on horseback and buggy, but Sam finally recognized the automotive store with the never-used batteries.

Telegraph systems typically put 50-150 volts on the telegraph line to transmit a signal, so the scouting party loaded the small buggy with fifteen 12-volt batteries and a large rack of dusty glass-lined bottles of acid that had been supplied with the batteries to charge them. Sam warned them to be careful with the acid as it was so corrosive, it could dissolve the skin on anyone unfortunate enough to spill it on themselves. Most acid bottles on the rack were empty but some still contained enough to charge a few batteries.

Back at the warehouse, Sam carefully added water to the batteries and then some acid and waited until the fumes coming out of the batteries stopped, then put the caps back on to seal them.

There were several dusty solar cell panels, and he spent some time cleaning them and hooking them up to the batteries and the telegraph devices. He took his flashlight out, cranked it, and shined the light onto the solar cells. The telegraphs hummed and clicked a few times. They seemed to be okay, so Arun and Sam decided to wait for daylight to charge the batteries enough to test the system over a short distance.

Chapter 12

ANA'S LEARNING

Ana was extremely bored waiting for Sam to return. She started with a few children's books, then read all the books she could find in his house in one day. The next day she returned to the large house Sam had shown her for her new home as it had a large library of books. Behind his house, she had found the cart he used to haul stuff from the hardware and food stores and quickly piled it high with books from the house's library. That should keep her busy for a while. Ana didn't know that she had a photographic memory with almost 100% retention until she realized she had read every book in the cart in only three more days. The only challenging books were a complete set of Encyclopedia Britannica and a Grey's Anatomy medical book.

Although she liked reading books she was bored again and headed to the clothing store to pick out a few more outfits. Later, at the nearby food store, she found an unopened stack of women's magazines still wrapped in plastic and was soon looking in the grocery's makeup section for anything that might still be usable. She even found some lipstick she liked. She looked in a mirror and wondered what Sam would think of her new look.

There was a constant threat of attack by wild animals and Ana became determined to find a more powerful weapon to defend herself. Sam had a few shotguns and rifles and she practiced with those behind the house, but she wanted something better.

One day, while looking around the former shopping center, she found a used bookstore and happened to find some shelves with books about military history and weapons. While she flipped through them, she wondered if Sam had been able to help the resistance.

She finally tired of waiting for him and became determined to find him and even join the resistance, if that were the only way she could be near him.

One the way back home, she tried a different route and found a former sporting goods store. The store had been ransacked and was almost empty but in a storeroom in the back of the store her flashlight illuminated a locked cabinet, sort of hidden in a dark corner of the storeroom. She shot the lock off and found a small but significant cache of weapons. She found a shopping cart in the store that still rolled easily and filled it with several rifles, shotguns, semi-automatic rifles and ammunition from the cabinet. She also found a book about cleaning guns and soon had a working semi-automatic rifle. The next day, it proved invaluable as she was confronted by a pack of wild hogs on the way home from the food store. She was amazed at how easy it was to disperse the pack with the semi-automatic rifle. After a day or so of practicing behind the house, she packed her knapsack with some clothes and other essentials, put in a semi-automatic rifle and some ammunition, slung it over her shoulder and set off to find Sam and the resistance.

It was late in the afternoon when she returned to the place Sam had been taken and it didn't take long to find the resistance. She saw someone dressed in camouflage and followed him back to the resistance's warehouse. A sentry challenged her, but she convinced him she was there to find Sam and join them if necessary. As he escorted her to Arun, she saw Sam and ran to him. Sam was shocked at her transformation with makeup and lipstick.

"Wow! You look great. I haven't seen a woman wearing makeup in years. Where did you find the makeup and lipstick?"

"I found some magazines and the makeup in the grocery store."

After a few hugs and kisses Sam showed her their working telegraph. They had been able to establish regular communications with the Baytown group and the groups were starting to work together to devise strategies for fighting the aliens.

She abruptly kicked him hard in the leg and he yelled. "What the hell was that for?"

"You said you would help them with communications and wouldn't be away from me a minute longer than you needed to be. It looks like you finished this some time ago."

Sam rubbed his leg and laughed. "You're right, but there is so much to do here, I sort of lost track of time."

"And forgot about me…"

She tried to kick him in the leg again, but he dodged her. "Ok, I'm sorry. I was just trying to help everyone here. I knew you were safe and could take care of yourself." He saw the semi-automatic rifle poking out of her knapsack. "Are you carrying an automatic rifle?"

"Semi-automatic. I've been practicing with it."

"Maybe you can help them with their weapons, then."

She looked at the weapons the resistance fighters had collected. They basically had the same weapons she had found in the sporting goods store, and she knew they would be no match for the advanced weapons the aliens undoubtedly had. Sam followed her as she walked over to Arun and introduced herself. Arun remembered her from when they forced Sam to help the resistance.

"You look different." *Better.* She wasn't bad before but now she was pretty hot. She sure looked like the girlfriend of the brother of one of the resistance members. He noticed Sam had put his arm around her waist.

"I've had a lot of time to fill."

Arun knew exactly what she meant as she continued.

"Just out of curiosity, have you ever tried to negotiate with the aliens?"

"Negotiate? What is there to negotiate?"

"Some kind of peace agreement, maybe? We leave them alone and they leave us alone, or something like that."

"I don't think anyone here wants that. They haven't attacked us yet, but we want them gone."

"They might be willing to share some technology with us…maybe help us get the power back on. Have you even tried to talk to them?"

"No one here as ever seen one. Not even a sentry at their encampment's perimeter fence. We did hear that the Baytown group contacted them and tried several times to negotiate. The aliens just laughed at them, until the Baytown guys ambushed a few aliens who had wandered outside their encampment. They weren't laughing then, but that also ended all negotiations. After that they started using some small spacecraft to patrol near their encampment during the day, looking for resistance groups. We don't know what they'll do if they find us."

Ana doubted that version of the encounter. Any intelligent species would want to avoid a conflict if possible. Maybe they were so advanced technologically, they weren't worried about a conflict with humans. She wondered if negotiations might be possible sometime in the future. For now, if she helped them, maybe she and Sam could go back home sooner.

"So, what's the plan?"

"We need to give them a reason to leave."

"Or, negotiate?"

"I think that's a pipedream, but OK."

"Any species that can travel through space probably has advanced weapons as well. Realistically, you can't hope to defeat them with the weapons you have today."

"I know, but if we could organize resistance groups near every encampment and harass them enough, they might decide staying isn't worth it and leave."

"Or negotiate?"

"Unlikely, but OK."

"In any case, you're going to need a lot more firepower it you ever hope to convince the aliens to leave or negotiate."

"I know. We've been to all the local sporting goods and gun stores, and this is the best we could find."

"What about a Texas Army National Guard armory?"

Arun just stared at her. "I was originally with the Guard in Compton, California. We don't have anyone here who knows where the nearest armory is. The city of Houston covers over 600 square miles, which makes it hard to find anything when you're on horseback or riding around in a buggy."

"I read a book written by a former member of the Texas guard. According to the map in the book, the nearest armory is probably 15 to 20 or so miles East from here, or about three to four hours by horseback."

"That's great! We can send a team there tomorrow to see what's still there."

"Why wait for tomorrow? If we leave now, we could be back by morning and could avoid possible alien patrols during the day."

Several resistance members had wandered over to listen to their conversation and verbally volunteered to go. They soon started packing some supplies for the trip.

Chapter 13

NATIONAL GUARD ARMORY

It wasn't easy to navigate in the dark with only a compass but after a few hours, they arrived at the former National Guard armory. At the main building, one team member broke a window, used a hacksaw on the bars on the window and climbed in to unlock the doors for the rest. The armory complex was huge, with numerous buildings spread over several acres. One team member complained that it could take all night to search the armory complex for weapons.

Ana replied, "We only need to find the vault."

After an hour of searching, they found the vault, but the enormous vault door had a keypad that required a code and without power the keypad's backup batteries were dead. How could they open the vault? It was obvious someone had tried and failed to open the lock on the vault door with a hacksaw. Ana wondered if that would make it impossible to open the door even if they could find a way to re-activate the door locking mechanism.

She turned to Sam. "We'll have to open it the hard way…"

He returned a few minutes later from the horse and buggy rolling a rack with an acetylene torch and gas cylinders to the vault.

"I hope this works, this is the last Acetylene tank we know about."

He put on a welder's helmet and started cutting into the locking mechanism. It soon fell off and she and Arun could manually turn the door's locking mechanism until it clicked. She motioned to the others to help, and they all tugged on the massive door as it slowly opened.

The vault was dark and dusty, but Ana shined her flashlight around and they found a huge number of weapons still on racks or in metal cabinets. Arun pointed to a rack of automatic rifles. Most of them were noticeably rusty, but Arun seemed excited.

"That's what I've been looking for." He noticed Ana shaking her head and suddenly realized why. "They won't be very effective over any real distance."

Ana shined her light on an automatic rifle and examined it. "You'll probably never get close enough to them to use it."

Arun sighed. "A sniper's rifle would be more effective, but no one has those skills anymore."

"Even a sniper wouldn't help. The aliens probably have advanced day and night vision systems, and they'll see you coming."

"So, what do we need then?"

Ana walked to a storage rack of large weapons and pointed to a box with an 81mm mortar launcher system. "That! You can hit them up to 4500 meters or about two and a half miles."

"Hit them?"

"We first have to get their attention, so whenever they are outside or land and open a door, shoot one of those mortars at the ship. It probably won't damage anything, but it will scare the hell out of them. The problem is these old-style mortars are not very accurate. The newest ones used to travel up to six miles, but we couldn't see the target at that distance. What we really need is an FGM-148 Javelin anti-tank rocket launcher or some TOW missiles, but we'll have to find a regular army base to get hold of those."

"How do you know so much about weapon systems?"

"I've read a lot of books." She waved her flashlight around and commented. "We have a bigger problem."

"What?"

"Most Army National Guard armories didn't store ammunition for their weapons. It was usually brought from the nearest regular army base when it was needed. There doesn't appear to be any small arms ammunition or mortar shells here."

The team searched the large vault until Arun kicked a rack. "Dammit. My Guard unit in Compton kept ammunition in their vault. What do we do now?"

"We'll have to find the nearest army or marine base and hope there is some still there."

One of the team commented. "I used to live in Austin. The Fort Hood army base was in Killeen, about 60 miles northeast of Austin. The Lackland Air Force Base was near San Antonio."

He made a sketch on the floor's dust, showing Houston, San Antonio, Austin and Killeen. Ana did some quick mental math and shook her head. "So, Killeen is a little over one hundred and seventy miles to the northwest of here and San Antonio is almost the same distance due west. By horseback, that's about four days each way to either base." She rubbed her rear. "My butt hurts just thinking about that ride." One day on a buggy from her parent's house to Katy had been bad enough.

Arun and a few of the team members laughed but they were thinking the same thing. "Let's take what we need here and worry about ammo and mortar shells tomorrow."

The team loaded several boxes of automatic rifles and mortar launcher systems onto a large cart pulled by two horses.

One of the team complained to Arun. "I can't see shit now. We should wait for daylight to go back."

"It's risky to travel at night because of the wild animals, but it's probably riskier to travel during the day, because of the aliens. We'll be fine if we stay on the roads."

It took most of the night, but they finally made it back to the warehouse just before dawn. The rest of the team admired their new haul of weapons until Arun updated them on the ammo problem. After breakfast, he pulled a digital camera out of a locker and motioned Ana to follow him. They walked outside into the sunlight, and he showed her some pictures of the electronic fence.

"How do you still have a working camera? I thought all batteries would be unusable by now."

"This was an experimental camera that used batteries and a small solar panel to charge the batteries. The batteries were dead when I found it, but the solar panel still trickle-charges the old Nickel Metal Hydride batteries just enough to take a few pictures when the sun is shining."

While she flipped through the pictures he continued. "The electronic fence looks like it will zap any living creature with some type of plasma. You can see through it, but everything beyond seems hazy, almost like a mirage. There doesn't seem to be a way around it."

"Could you tunnel under it?"

"Possibly, but it would take a long time and the fence may have some sensors that would detect a tunnel being dug under it. We really don't know much about it."

"Let's go see it. The mortar idea may still work if we can find some shells. How far is the fence from the ship or main encampment?"

"When you climb a tree and look over the fence the encampment seems pretty far, several miles, I think. It looks like they are starting to plant crops or something like that inside the fence line."

"Mortars may not have the accuracy we need if we have to fire beyond the fence. We can test them once we find some mortar shells."

Two people approached Arun and he tapped Ana on the shoulder to get her attention. "I think you need to meet these guys."

Ana turned and stared in disbelief as one of them was her older sister that she hadn't seen in years. Camila and her boyfriend were both wearing green and brown camouflage clothing and Camila's hair was tucked up inside a hunting hat.

Ana let out a screech that surprised everyone. "Camila!" Ana ran to hug her sister. Everyone left them alone while they hugged and chatted excitedly, trying to catch each other up on their time apart until Camila introduced Ana to Robert, her boyfriend. He was surprised at Ana's clothing and makeup as was Camila, something neither had seen in a while. "You have to show me where you found your clothes and makeup."

They left to find Camila some new clothes, and makeup of course.

Sam came looking for Ana and Arun told him about Ana's reunion with Camila and introduced him to Robert.

Later that afternoon, Ana and Camila returned wearing new outfits and makeup. Robert was amazed at Camila's new look. Even Sam noticed that Ana had a new outfit and different makeup. The sisters and their boyfriends found an empty table and sat down to discuss their lives and relationships, their hopes for the future and eventually how they could help the resistance.

While Arun and some team members were making plans for a long and difficult road trip to find ammunition, they received some exciting news from the Baytown resistance group. Ana was eating dinner at the communal table with Sam, Camila and Robert when Arun entered and made an announcement.

"The Baytown resistance group was in the old Exxon refinery two days ago and found a gasoline tank about three quarters full. They want us to come and help them figure out the best way to use it."

Ana glanced at Sam across the dinner table and commented in a low tone. "It's probably useless as a fuel."

Arun overheard her and confronted her. "Why is it useless?"

Almost every eye was on her now, so she had to answer. "That tank had to be open to the atmosphere to prevent it from building up pressure when it gets hot. There probably was a Nitrogen purge when it was in use to keep the air out, but that's been gone for years. Over those years, gasoline in an open tank will have lost most of its light ends and will have absorbed a lot of water and bacteria from the air."

"So, what?"

"Water will form a layer at the bottom of the tank and the bacteria will thrive at the interface between the water and the gasoline. Over time they will change the gasoline to a much thicker material almost like turpentine, and with no light ends, it will plug up any gasoline engine you put it in."

Arun wasn't buying her argument. "How do you know this?"

"I read a lot"

Robert leaned toward Camila and whispered, "how does your sister know all this?"

"I don't know. She always was a fast learner."

Sam laughed. "So, is there anything we can do to make it useful again?"

Ana noticed everyone waiting for an answer. "We'd have to distill it again, somehow."

Arun wandered over to stand next to her. "Is that possible?"

Ana thought for a minute. "Anything we could use for that in the refinery will probably be rusted beyond repair." Then it came to her. "But we might be able to do something like the distillation process that moonshiners used to do."

One of the older resistance fighters knew exactly what she was talking about and jumped to his feet. "That's a great idea! It would be worth doing even if we only wound up with a way to make some real booze."

Everyone laughed until Arun tapped a spoon against a drinking glass. "Can you tell the rest of us what the hell you are talking about?"

"Moonshiners used to make a crude alcohol from corn mash, water and yeast. When the fermentation step was done, they had to use a distillation step to separate the alcohol from the rest of the mixture." She chuckled. "They used to do that at night in the forest where they wouldn't be found by government tax agents who were always trying to find them. That's where the term 'moonshiner' comes from. I also read they stacked radiators from cars in junkyards to do the distillation in plain sight. That put them closer to buyers in the cities. Are there any automobile junkyards near here?"

Everyone was silent for a moment, until one member stood up. "I know where one is. It's not too far from here."

Arun looked at Sam. "Can you lead a small group there and see if Ana can find what she needs? I'll contact Baytown and tell them what we are trying to do."

Ana cautioned him. "Make sure they only draw off gasoline at the top of the tank. That's the farthest from the water and bacteria. And… ask them to try and find a tank with diesel. Diesel is much heavier and probably not as affected by the bacteria in a water layer. Diesel trucks would be more useful than gasoline cars anyway."

Arun nodded and headed off to the telegraph room.

Sam turned to Ana. "How about going now, before it gets dark?"

"Sure. Why don't we just take a few carts and some tools and bring back what we need?"

"Let's do it!" Several resistance team members were bored with the lack of anything productive to do and volunteered to help them. Robert and Camila left the group to find some new things from a list Arun had given them.

A short while later, the small convoy of horse drawn carts pulled into an old automobile junkyard and the team started wandering around looking for radiators that weren't too rusty. They found several and soon were heading back to the resistance headquarters.

It didn't take long to stack the radiators and an old water heater into a crude distillation system at the back of the converted warehouse. Ana watched as Sam welded the radiator connections together. "Now all we need is some gasoline."

Chapter 14

MUSIC

Ana was bored waiting for the gasoline from the Baytown group. She wandered around the warehouse until she found a pile of electronics the group had gathered from an electronics store in case power was ever restored. Ana didn't know what most of it was and was examining a music "boombox" when Sam wandered over to see what she was doing. "What are you doing?"

She held up the boombox. "What is this?"

"It was called a boombox. Basically, it played music from disks or memory devices. It would be great if we could power it somehow. There's a pile of CDs and DVDs here." He pointed to a stack of silver disks and boxes of DVDs.

"CDs?"

"Compact Disks. They held about a dozen songs. Usually by the same group or singer. When smart phones came along, everyone started storing their music on their phones and CDs and dedicated music players just sort of faded away."

"Do you still have a smart phone?"

"Everyone had one until the power went out, the cell networks went down and there was no way to recharge them. I probably lost mine or gave it away, I can't remember. I haven't seen a cell phone in years."

"OK, what about these CD players? Couldn't we charge them from the solar cells?"

"Most solar panels only had a 20-year lifetime and the ones we have are probably that old, so they don't put out much current anymore." He saw a digital music player. "If we could find some rechargeable batteries, we might get this to work. This doesn't need much power."

The team had taken the batteries out of most of the electronics so they wouldn't corrode further and ruin the device. Most electronic devices that were ruined by corroded batteries had been tossed into a scrap pile in a corner of the warehouse. Sam spotted a pair of rechargeable batteries in a pile of removed batteries.

"These are rechargeable!" He put the batteries in the music player and connected several solar panels to recharge them. A small red light came on the player. "It's working but it could take a while. These old solar cells don't generate much power now."

After lunch they returned to the player and Sam put some earplugs in her ears and turned the player on.

Sam laughed as it seemed that Ana was mesmerized by the music as she had heard very little music most of her life other than the music she learned to play by ear on her guitar.

They took turns listening to the player for a while until he told Ana he needed to go back home and check on a few things while they waited for the fuel from the Baytown group. Ana kissed him and watched him walk off through the woods. She then put on some headphones and listened to the digital music player while she looked through the pile of CDs.

She became bored with that and found Arun to develop a plan to confront the aliens. After a brief chat about possible ways to contact the aliens, they were sitting at the dining table and some salt and pepper shakers on the table reminded Ana of some chess pieces. She asked Arun if he played chess or checkers. He said he was an internationally ranked chess player back in California.

Ana immediately asked him if he had a chess set. Surprisingly, he did, and he eagerly accepted her challenge to a game. They played for a while and Arun won the first game easily, but barely won the second, and Ana won the third. Arun was surprised.

"Where did you learn to play chess?"

"My dad showed me the basic game, but he wasn't very good. Sam and I played a lot at night after dinner."

Arun shook his head. "I haven't been beaten by a non-ranked player in a long time."

Ana was thinking out loud. "Are there other team members that play? Maybe we could have a tournament."

"I think so, but I would have to find a few more chess sets if we have a tournament."

Ana thought of Camila. "Maybe Camila and Robert could find us some."

Arun nodded. "They were asking if there was anything else they could find for us. I'll ask them."

Ana watched him write a list of things they needed to ask Camila to look for and wondered out loud. "Sounds like you spent a lot of time in California. How did you wind up in Texas?"

He smiled. "I was visiting a friend in Houston when the meteor shower happened. Unfortunately, I waited a few days to go back and then it was too late as everyone seemed to forget how to drive and there were accidents everywhere. I called my girlfriend and told her I would be here a little while longer until it became safe to drive and she told me 'don't bother coming back'. I asked her why and she told me she found out my 'friend' here was female. My friend then invited me to stay here until it became less dangerous to travel, or as long as I wanted. It never became safe, and I never wanted to go back, so here I am."

Ana chuckled. "What happened to the 'friend' you stayed with?"

Arun shrugged. "She left with some other girlfriends to find a better life, somewhere in the northern part of Houston. At least that's what she said."

That triggered a memory in Ana. "Was one of her girlfriends the daughter of a farmer near Katy?"

Arun seemed surprised. "How could you possibly know that?"

"Sam lives near a farmer and his daughter used to be his girlfriend until she decided to leave with some girlfriends to live in northern Houston."

Arun seemed shocked. "Wow, what are the odds of that?"

Ana laughed, then told Arun how her parents found a remote house just west of Sealy hoping it would be safer there. "And here we are."

Arun laughed.

Two days later, Sam returned just before two members of the Baytown resistance team arrived with a horse drawn cart loaded with two barrels of gasoline. Sam poured some into a glass container – it was thick and cloudy and smelled rancid – not like the smell of gasoline that he remembered.

Ana cautioned him. "That's probably too far gone for a simple distillation. It would probably take a multi-plate distillation tower, like they used to have in the refinery, for it to work."

Sam held up a glass container of the murky gasoline to a light. "Let's give it a try, anyway."

They tried a simple one-pass distillation that failed as the gasoline was still thick and cloudy and not useful as a fuel for cars. A few days later they received two barrels of diesel from the same resistance group. This time, when they poured some into a glass container it had a lot of floating particles in it, but it was almost clear and colorless.

Ana glanced at Sam. "This looks promising."

She watched Sam filter the diesel through several automobile oil filters into three five-gallon fuel cans and pour it into a truck's fuel tank. "Now we just need to find a usable heavy-duty battery to crank this diesel engine over."

All the resistance members were aware that lead acid batteries typically used in cars and trucks have a very limited storage life of two to five years. After 15 years of sitting in a strong acid solution, the internal metal electrodes were practically gone, and the batteries could not be charged again.

"What about the telegraph batteries?" asked Arun. "Can we use them?"

Sam thought about that. "Perhaps, but they're really intended to put voltage on the telegraph line, not a lot of current, so we don't have to charge them much with the solar cells. An old diesel engine probably needs 500 or more amps just to crank it over. It would take a really long time to fully charge those batteries from the solar cells we have. They're pretty old and they just don't put out enough current anymore."

It suddenly came to him. "A diesel generator could charge the battery."

"Do you have one?"

"No, but hardware stores usually sold generators. Most of them were probably built to use gasoline or propane or natural gas, so it may not be easy to find one built for diesel. But there are probably half a dozen hardware stores within a day's horse ride from here."

"Let's go looking tomorrow."

It took almost a week, but with four teams looking, they finally found a farm goods hardware store with a diesel generator. It was heavy, but together they managed to lift it onto a horse drawn cart.

Back in the encampment, it only took a day for Sam to checkout and overhaul the generator. The generator could be started by a hand-crank similar to a lawnmower and all the resistance members were gathered around the generator and cheered when it finally coughed and started. Sam had hooked it to the warehouse power, and everyone cheered when the lights came on, something they had not seen in more than 10 years. They quickly turned off most of the lights to avoid possible detection by the aliens and to reduce the load on the generator. Sam connected a 12volt power converter to the generator to charge the truck battery and they left to celebrate.

The next morning Sam quickly installed the newly charged battery in a flatbed truck and Ana held her breath as Sam turned the key and the engine slowly cranked over. It sputtered some but finally started to the cheers of the small crowd of resistance fighters that had gathered to watch.

Sam drove the truck around the warehouse a few times and then stopped to let Ana in. They drove all the way to the former interstate highway and Sam floored it. Ana held on tightly as Sam veered around large potholes and rusted hulks of cars and trucks. When they finally returned to the encampment, everyone gathered around to hear the results.

Arun was elated. He said they could finally move about easily and find what they needed and help other resistance groups in the fight against the aliens.

At an evening campfire, Arun confessed he had almost lost hope several times and that the diesel discovery, simple distillation and recharging of the lead acid battery and subsequently getting a truck running had given him new hope for their survival.

Ana wondered how other resistance groups were doing. "Have you even been to the Baytown group's headquarters?"

Arun nodded. "Why do you want to know?"

"You said your goal was to harass the aliens enough to make them leave. I was just wondering how the other groups are doing in convincing the aliens to leave."

"They are about where we were when we asked Sam to help us." Arun addressed the whole group gathered around the campfire. "I just wanted to acknowledge the help that Ana and Sam have been to us. I know we sort of forced you to help us, but we really weren't making much progress in our goal of trying to convince the aliens to leave and we needed all the help we could get to keep going. So, thanks again."

Sam and Ana nodded to the applause of the team.

That started a whole new discussion on the future until Ana reminded them, they still needed to find some ammunition if they ever wanted to attack the aliens to get their attention.

Chapter 15

AMMUNITION

Although it was risky traveling by day, they opted to look in an army base first and the field trip to the Fort Hood Army Base in Killeen took only four hours in the truck on an interstate highway instead of four days by horseback. The first vault they found, and were able to open with an acetylene torch, held a significant cache of small arms ammo and mortar shells. They piled as much ammunition in the flatbed of the truck as it could carry and headed back home. The whole trip took only a day instead of weeks. Ana watched as Arun removed a mortar system from several crates and started assembling it.

"We need to test the concept. How about along the old interstate? We could use the mile markers to see how far we can shoot a mortar shell – if the launcher systems still work."

The next day a small group tested a mortar system and on maximum distance, it surprisingly traveled about three miles and then exploded on impact.

Arun lowered his binoculars. "Ok, so I think it's worth a try…"

Two days later, Ana had her first look at the alien encampment's electronic fence. The metal fenceposts were about 12 feet high and spaced about 10 feet apart. There was a slight blue glow around each fencepost and a very light blue glow between the fenceposts. Arun picked up a stick and threw it between two fenceposts. The blue glow between the posts quickly became stronger and the stick was fried as it neared the fence line. Arun threw another stick at a fencepost, but it was fried before it could actually hit the fencepost. Arun warned Ana not to get too close.

"Be careful. We've seen that fence fry a large hog that ventured too closely. At night, the glow between the fenceposts is a lot more visible."

The hazy blue glow of the fence kept her from seeing the actual encampment in the distance. She tried looking through some high-powered binoculars without success. "How can we see the main buildings."

"We have to climb." He pointed to a tall nearby tree and helped her climb onto a lower branch. He managed to scramble up the tree and followed her as she climbed higher.

She waited for Arun near the top of the tree and commented. "I haven't climbed a tree since I was a little girl."

"I haven't climbed a tree since I was in good shape."

He was out of breath and panting from the exertion. They both pulled out their high-powered binoculars from small knapsacks and observed the activity in the encampment. A large silver spaceship was central to the encampment, but numerous small buildings had been set up immediately around the ship. A few small sentry buildings were scattered along the fence and the door to the ship seemed to be open most of the time. There were no sentries in sight.

Arun complained. "I can't get a good estimate of the distance."

Ana had a suggestion. "We could triangulate." Arun just stared at her.

On the way back to the warehouse, Ana asked Arun about guards. "I didn't see any sentries. Has anyone here ever seen a guard or a sentry at the fence?"

Arun thought for a moment. "No one ever mentioned seeing one."

"Then how did the Baytown group make contact to talk to them?"

"I don't know. Maybe that was just a story they made up so we would want to work with them."

When they were nearing the warehouse, Ana remembered the need to measure the distance from the fence to the ship. "Does anyone know of someone that might have some engineering surveying tools, so we can measure the distance to the ship from the fence?"

"Camila's boyfriend, Robert might. He once said his father was a civil engineer and Robert might have some of his dad's equipment. I'll check with him."

Robert happened to be in the warehouse when they returned, and he said his father had something that might work – for a price of course (food).

When Robert left, Arun surprised Ana with an acoustic guitar (with all its strings). "I asked Robert to keep an eye out for a guitar. Sam once told me you used to play the guitar." He handed her some sheet music. "He also found this."

Arun then showed her a stack of chess sets. "They found these in an old toy store. I guess there are other things more important to most people these days."

Lastly, he handed her a watercolor paint set and two small canvases. "Sam told me you liked to paint. So, I asked Camila and she found these."

Ana was so surprised and happy, she hugged Arun. If she hadn't been in a relationship with Sam, she might have been open to one with Arun. They still disagreed on how to confront the aliens but agreed on many other things. They did agree to set up a chess tournament when enough people expressed an interest in one. They even agreed that Ana could paint a portrait of the tournament winner as the grand prize.

Robert returned the next day with a knapsack filled with engineering surveying and drafting tools. Ana searched through the bag until she held up a surveying measuring tape. She couldn't help but notice all the equipment in the bag bore the logo of a German surveying company. Robert said his father worked in Germany for many years before he came to Houston.

Ana found the angle measuring tools she needed. "This is exactly what we need."

Robert left happy with several packages of prepper food, while Ana and Arun returned to the trees nearest the alien encampment's electronic fence.

"These instruments are all calibrated in the metric system, so we'll need to find two trees about 300 meters apart, or roughly 1000 feet."

They soon found two suitable trees and used the surveying tape to measure the distance between them. Ana climbed one tree while Arun climbed the other. He held up a small mirror as a reference point and Ana measured the angle to the spaceship. They then swapped places and she measured the angle to the ship from the other tree. Back at the warehouse, Arun gave her a solar-powered calculator and she calculated the distance to the ship. When she finished, she shook her head and sighed.

"What's wrong?"

"The ship is almost 5000 meters from the fence, or a little over three miles. Unfortunately, the accuracy of the mortar system is only 137 meters at that distance. That's about 450 feet, or about three times as the length of the warehouse."

"How could you possibly know that?"

"I found a manual for the mortar at Fort Hood."

Arun wasn't willing to give up at this point. "Let's try it anyway. If we can meet them and get inside that ship, we might be able to find some weaknesses we could exploit."

Ana sighed. "I wish we could just try to talk to them about a peace treaty."

"How can we do that if there are no sentries or guards to ask? You know, no one has ever seen one."

Ana shrugged. "I guess we have to get their attention first."

When they returned to the camp, Arun filled in the resistance group with the latest plan on using the mortar to get the aliens to leave or just get their attention. Afterwards, Sam expressed his concern to Arun on the possible risks.

"This seems like an excessive way to convince them to leave, or even meet them to talk about a peace agreement as Ana wants to do. They could retaliate and just kill the mortar team or all of us."

"What else can we do? They probably don't even know we exist."

Sam sighed. "I hope they don't shoot first and ask questions later."

"That's why I told the others we need to run away after the attack, so they will chase and catch us, otherwise if we just stand there, they could do just that."

Sam shook his head. "I just hope this plan works."

Ana sighed. "What else can we do? We can't continue on like this forever. What's left in the grocery stores and that prepper food won't last that much longer, and someday all the people that know how to grow crops, like your farmer neighbor, will be gone. Then what will be do?"

Sam wished he had an alternate plan but couldn't come up with anything. "I guess you're right. Waiting them out isn't an option."

Chapter 16

MORTAR ATTACK

After practicing on the interstate for most of the morning, Arun felt they were ready. Normally, an 81mm mortar team was comprised of five people but for this attack Arun felt they only needed Sam and three other members, as Ana and Arun would be watching the results from their treetop perches. The sun was just setting as they launched a dozen mortar shells at the ship. Most missed badly but one exploded in the open doorway. The team abandoned the launch system and hurried back into the woods.

Arun and Ana were watching the results with binoculars from high up in a tree and Ana gave Arun a "thumbs up" sign. They quickly climbed down and hurried to rejoin the others.

Arun laughed when Ana commented, "I think we got their attention now!"

Alien Reaction

The shock wave from the mortar shell that landed in the doorway injured more than a dozen and shocked everyone in the camp. The fence that was supposed to stop animals or possible humans had not stopped the mortar attack.

The site immediately went on high alert and launched several small scout ships.

A bright light flashed overhead before the resistance group could return to their base. Arun yelled "Damn! Run!" The group scattered through the woods, but Ana didn't get very far before she noticed a strange chemical smell. She lost consciousness and fell to the ground.

Advanced heat detection technology had enabled the aliens to easily find Ana and Arun's resistance group. They captured six resistance fighters (three females and three males) and transported them to a small building just inside the fence to determine who the leader was, and why they had attacked the encampment. Surprisingly, several aliens spoke English and began to question them individually as they woke up.

Arun immediately declared that he was the leader, but after cross-examining him, they decided that despite his obvious military knowledge, he didn't seem smart enough to develop high level strategies and then started examining Sam. They also dismissed him as the leader as he also seemed to lack the high-level skills needed to plan strategies. Who was the leader then? They quickly interviewed the last male without success.

The aliens had questioned all the men first and reported back to their patrol team leader that they couldn't identify the high-level planner. The team leader asked them if they questioned the women and the three questioners just laughed. The leader reprimanded them and told them to interview everyone.

Ana woke up and immediately realized she was in an alien vessel or building. The walls, ceiling and floor were metal and electronic displays practically covered the walls. The three resistance women had apparently been separated from the men. One was awake like Ana, sitting against a wall and the other was unconscious on the floor.

There was a loud discussion outside the door and three male aliens entered. From the insignia on their silver uniforms and their demeanor, Ana assumed they were soldiers. They motioned for the other woman to come over to a table with chairs and began questioning her. Ana knew they were recording the interviews when she saw an image of the woman on a display near her. She heard them ask about the resistance: who was the leader, how many members were there, what weapons did they have, what were the group's goals, and so on. The woman named Arun as the leader but was vague on the rest. The aliens had already examined Arun and were convinced he was not the strategic planner.

The other woman was awake by then and they questioned her next with Ana last. This was her first close contact with the aliens. Although the aliens were similar to humans, Ana could easily see the difference. Their skin was a light orange color and they had large dark eyes, small ears and nose but a humanlike mouth. There were variations in their hair color, and all three seemed muscular. She did notice that all three interrogators seemed to be staring at her chest before one of them started questioning her. When they asked about leadership, she gave them Arun's name knowing he wouldn't be able to help them much. He had practical combat knowledge but little planning skills. Based on the depth of her answers, the interrogators suspected Ana knew more than she was letting on.

After all the women gave Arun's name, the investigating team leader was frustrated at their attempt to hide the true leader. Although he didn't have the authority to do it, he told the women they would start executing the men one by one until someone identified the true strategist. That was unexpected and Ana didn't know if the interrogation team would, or could do that, but she felt compelled to admit she was the planner. They let most of the captives go by deactivating a section of the fence and told her that she and Arun would be taken to a higher-level leader for further questioning. She was separated from Arun and transported in a small open vehicle to a central building in the encampment. It was not all that different than a golf cart. There were several golf carts in the resistance warehouse that they early on had stripped of their batteries as they tried to get the telegraph machines to work (unsuccessfully).

Ana noticed how quiet the small open cart was, compared to the flat-bed diesel truck Sam had revived. She wondered if it was powered by a solar-powered electric motor or perhaps some more advanced form of energy.

Her interrogation team led her to a small room in the building. They seemed to be waiting for someone and motioned her to sit in a chair. She had an electromagnetic handcuff device on that was uncomfortably tight. A female alien wearing a metallic uniform with a yellow collar and several yellow stripes on her sleeves entered and all the soldiers came to attention – Ana assumed she must be someone important. Unlike the muscular male soldiers, the female leader was tall and slender. Her hair was longer and much lighter than the male soldiers, almost blond. Her eyes were also lighter, almost hazel in color. Her skin was a very light shade of orange.

The handcuffs were bothering her, so Ana asked the new leader. "Do you understand me?

One of her questioners leaned near her and whispered. "Do not question the lieutenant. Only answer her questions."

Lieutenant? She repeated her question louder. The lieutenant had been discussing the results so far with the lead interrogator in their native language but looked at her.

"Yes, I understand…English."

"Can you take these off? They hurt. I won't try to escape."

The nearest questioner pushed her from the back. "Silence!"

The lieutenant said something to the lead interrogator, and he motioned to the nearest interrogator to take the handcuffs off. Once they were off, Ana rubbed her wrists.

"That's better."

The new leader had seen a recording of the questioning of the six captives, but this was the first female she had seen personally. Ana had come a long way since she left her remote cabin (stylish clothes, makeup and some jewelry – she also combed her hair and wore hats). The other human females she had seen in the video interviews were wearing fatigues and caps and not very attractive. She studied Ana for a moment. "What's your name?"

"Ana Cordoba. What's your name?"

The leader laughed and said, "Lieutenant Sarah Long".

Ana laughed as it seemed extremely unlikely, she would have such a name. "No, really?"

Long frowned. "Yes?" She paused, staring at Ana for a moment. "You are young, to be so knowledgeable."

"I've read a lot of books. By the way, what's your species name?"

"Species?"

"We call ourselves humans."

"Oh. We are Tribanis"

She wasn't sure she heard her correctly. "Tribanis?"

"Yes."

"What happened to our leader, Arun?"

"He has been extensively interrogated and does not seem to have much useful information. He will likely be released soon. We need to know more about your group, and our site security leader has instructed us to bring you to him for further questioning."

A soldier started to put the electronic handcuffs on, and Ana objected.

"You won't need that. I promise I won't try to escape. That kind of hurts."

The lieutenant waved away the soldier and they all walked a short distance to the central spaceship. The spaceship was enormous, but all Ana saw were endless corridors with countless closed doors. Every Tribani they passed, stopped, and stared at Ana as they had never seen a human before.

The interrogation team led her to a small room with a single bed and a connecting bathroom that had something like a shower and something that resembled a toilet. There was a miniature version of the electronic fence just outside the door, effectively making the room a small jail cell. Ana could close the door but not leave. Except for the bed the room was barren, and she paced for a while until she sighed and sat on the bed. She wished she at least had her knapsack or a change of clothes. She lost track of time and was so bored she stretched out on the bed and drifted off to sleep.

As soon as Sam and the other members of the mortar team were released, they hurried to the warehouse to inform the remaining resistance members of their capture and eventual release. All expressed concern for Ana and Arun. There wasn't anything they could do but wait to hear from them.

The next morning, Arun returned and was warmly greeted by everyone. He really couldn't add much to Sam's account of their capture and eventual release. From his perspective the mortar attack had worked. He was able to look at the alien's defenses, and security protocols. When pressed by Sam, he had to admit he really didn't learn anything that would allow them to harass the aliens enough to want to leave. They all hoped Ana could succeed in some sort of peace agreement.

Some time passed before Lieutenant Long and two soldiers appeared to take Ana to the site security leader. On the way, they stopped at what she assumed was a large lunchroom with several buffet type tables. She followed Long's example and filled a plate with something that smelled good and vaguely resembled scrambled eggs. The only utensil was similar to a spoon and even though she had no idea what the food was, or that it had almost no taste, she ate everything on her plate. One of her guards brought her a cup of water. When they had finished, they led her to a conference room with a table and chairs. Another male alien wearing a metallic uniform with a blue collar and several blue stripes on his sleeves was waiting for them. He motioned to her and Long to sit down on the opposite side of the table. The two guards took up sentry type duty outside the room. Her initial interview had seemed to drag on for hours and she wondered what else they could possibly ask her.

Although he had apparently reviewed her interview on an electronic tablet in front of him on the table the new leader began by asking her some of the same questions they had already asked.

"Ana Cordoba, my name is Captain John Morrison. I am responsible for the security of this base camp. We know you are the strategic planner for the group that attacked us yesterday."

Ana was listening carefully and made a mental note of his service rank. The titles of lieutenant and captain couldn't be a coincidence. She also noticed he used the word "yesterday" when describing her group's attack.

"Why did you attack us?"

"We wanted to get your attention."

Captain Morrison and Lieutenant Long looked at each other and both laughed. Morrison continued "for what purpose?"

From what Ana had seen or experienced so far, the resistance group's chance of defeating them was practically zero, so she tried a different tact.

"We would like to negotiate a peace agreement of some sort."

That seemed to surprise Morrison. "What does that mean?"

"Some of us have figured out that you were probably behind the meteor shower that released a chemical that resulted in most people losing their memories. You probably were surprised that some humans survived and didn't expect to meet any resistance when you came to colonize our planet."

Morrison and Long glanced at each other and Ana guessed that she had surprised them by her analysis of the meteor shower event.

Long started to shake her head. "We were not responsible for the meteor shower."

It was Ana's turn to look shocked. "What do you mean? Then who was responsible?"

Morrison replied. "There is another species that did this. We only found out about it after it happened."

Long folded her arms. "It some ways it's effects are worse for us."

Ana was still in shock. "Then why are you here? It must have taken a long time to prepare for the trip here and to prepare for living on Earth."

Long seemed eager to answer. "We have been preparing for a very long time to live here but were planning to blend in with humans in small colonies. We were not planning on living in a transport ship surrounded by a barrier that protects us from animals and humans."

"I don't understand." Ana was still confused. "What happened 15 years ago? Why do you speak English? Where are you from?"

Morrison interrupted. "This is outside my area of responsibility – security for the site."

Long suggested another source. "Sir, why don't we contact the remembrance official. I'm sure he could answer all of Ana's questions better than we could."

Morrison seemed to think about that, then nodded. "I will contact him. You will remain here until we can arrange for a meeting, just in case you are actually here to find possible weaknesses that your group can use to attack us."

Ana laughed as that was Arun's role.

Morrison got up to leave then stopped by the door and looked back. "What did you mean by a peace agreement?"

"I think most rational humans realize they can't defeat you, so they would like to cause you so many problems you would want to leave. I know now that doesn't seem very likely, so I would rather find a way for us to work together somehow."

"How could we work together?"

"You could help us restore the power system to start. That would make our lives much easier. We both could work on planting crops to improve our food supplies if we didn't have to worry about being attacked all the time. There are probably other ways we could help each other."

Morrison folded his arms thinking. "What groups do you represent? Would other humans be willing to form an agreement like this? We have been attacked by humans at several base camps and even by another group on the opposite side of this base camp. They appear to be a different group than yours."

"They could be willing to join once the benefits of an agreement are explained to them."

Morrison said something to Long in their native language and then turned to Ana. "I need to meet with our Advisory Council about this." He left and Lieutenant Long took Ana back to her small room.

Before she left her, Long commented. "I am sorry, but it could take some time before the Advisory Council meets and makes a possible decision on a peace agreement."

"If that's true, could you take me to a place where I can get some more clothes and some other things I need."

Long stared at her for a moment. "I will try to find some clothes for you, but it may not be possible because your shape is so different."

"There are other things I need as well."

Long knew what she meant and nodded. "I will contact the captain about this."

Later that day, Long escorted Ana to the dining hall. After two days, the routine (all day in her room, escorted by Long three times a day to the dining hall) was already starting to depress her. She hoped the routine wouldn't go on too much longer. She complained to Long who said she would discuss it with Captain Morrison.

Chapter 17

PRIVATE WILSON

The next day, Lieutenant Long stopped by with a new guard.

"Captain Morrison has agreed to let you out of your cell with a suitable guard, to ensure you won't try to escape. Private Wilson can escort you around the ship, but you cannot go outside at this time."

Ana stared at Wilson. He was pretty much like every other guard, but Ana was so bored, any change would be welcome. Long left and Wilson turned off the electronic barrier to her room. He motioned her to come out of the cell. He was wearing a weapon of some sort, but not carrying it.

"Hi, I'm Ana. What's your name?"

"Private Arthur Wilson." He hesitated. "It is almost time for the morning meal. Would you like to go now?"

There wasn't anything else to do, so Ana said "Yes."

He escorted her to the dining hall and they both filled their plates with the same bland yellow food they always had and then sat at a table. Ana noticed a few people staring at them but ignored the stares. Instead, she found herself staring at Wilson as he ate. "Is this the only food you eat?"

He seemed confused at the question. "Yes?"

"What is it, exactly?"

"I only know what I have read. It is made from a plant called Madjuul. A long time ago, the plant was modified so that it contains everything we need to live."

Ana stared at the lump of yellow food on her plate. "It's pretty tasteless."

"I'm not sure what you mean."

"Humans eat many different kinds of foods to get everything needed to live."

"I tried human food once. It was not good."

"You probably haven't tasted food that's been properly prepared."

Wilson shook his head. "I don't know what that means. Would you like to walk around? There are a few areas where only workers are allowed but there are many areas that you are allowed to visit."

The ship was vast, but all Ana could see were endless corridors of closed doors. After a while she said she was bored and asked Wilson to escort her back to her room. On the way back, she asked "Do all Tribanis speak English?"

"Everyone must learn to read English, but not all speak it. All security personnel must learn to speak it as well as a part of our training."

Later that day, when Wilson took her to the dining hall for the midday meal, she was bored and tried to learn more about him.

"Do you have family here?"

"No, I have some family at another base. When my duty is done here, I will go to them." He stared at her for a moment. "Do all human females look and dress as you do?"

That surprised her for a moment. "No, for some reason most of them seem to dress all alike, in hunting clothes."

"Hunting clothes?"

"Green and brown clothing that people wear to hunt and kill animals."

He seemed shocked. "You kill animals?"

"Yes, for food."

He was almost speechless. "You eat animals?"

She smiled at his expression. "Yes, but after they are prepared and cooked of course."

He dropped his spoon-like utensil, obviously upset.

"I guess you've never eaten fish, either."

"Fish?"

"Animals that swim in large bodies of water."

He just shook his head, too upset to continue eating.

"Surely, there must have been animals on Tribanus."

"A long time ago. The surface is now too hot for anything to live outside."

"Did you have any pets?"

"Pets?"

"Animals you keep and take care of for their company."

Wilson just stared at her for a moment. "We have no pets."

Ana shrugged and continued eating the mostly tasteless yellow food on her plate.

After a while, she noticed Wilson staring at her chest and wondered what he was thinking. She also wondered why he was armed.

"Why are you wearing a weapon?"

"What do you mean?"

"This site is surrounded by a protective fence, so why do you need to be armed?"

Wilson seemed confused at the question. "All members of the security service are required to wear their assigned protection."

"But why?"

Wilson struggled to find an answer. "It's a part of our uniform, in case we are ordered to leave the site."

This wasn't going anywhere, and she dropped that line of questioning.

Later that evening, when Wilson returned to escort her to the dining hall, she tried a different tactic. "Where are the children, I haven't seen any."

Wilson hesitated, he had been ordered not to divulge any security or military facts, but this seemed innocent enough. "During the day, they are instructed in one of the buildings near this vessel. At night they are with their…" He struggled with the term, so Ana volunteered "parents?"

Wilson nodded. "Yes. Their parents."

She wasn't sure she should ask but she did. "Do you have children?"

He laughed. "I am only 120000 sones now and not old enough to cause children or take care of them."

Ana didn't understand that time reference. It seemed like an odd answer as she would have guessed him to be the same age as the other guards, or even Lieutenant Long. She decided to drop that topic for now.

One of the small open carts passed them and she wished the resistance group had had something like that. She didn't like riding in horse-drawn buggies or riding on horseback the few times she had tried it. She sometimes saw the small carts entering and exiting the ship. She wondered if Wilson knew anything about them. She pointed at the cart.

"What kind of power source do those carts use."

Wilson stared after the cart for a moment. "I'm not sure. I think they run on water."

"How can they run on water?"

"I don't know."

She wanted to know more about them, but Wilson had already started walking back to her room, so she dropped it.

Each day Wilson, or another soldier who looked very much like him, would stop by her room three times to take her to the dining hall and then ask if she wanted to walk around. After a few days of endless hallways and closed doors, Ana declined the standard invitation to walk except after the evening meal.

The next time Wilson was on duty, she passed an open door and noticed a room with comfortable chairs. "Could we sit here for a while?"

"Yes, if you wish."

They settled in their chairs and Ana again noticed Wilson staring at her chest. That reminded her that she had never seen any public displays of affection, even while walking around after the evening meal. She was going to ask him if he was married, but decided he might not want to discuss that, so she tried another topic.

"What do you do for fun?"

"Fun?"

"Things you do when you are not on duty, with your friends."

He still seemed confused, so she added… "like sports or games or just enjoying the company of other people."

"I don't know what you mean."

"No sports or games?"

"No."

She was going to ask about drinking with friends, but he suddenly stood up. "I must ensure you are in your room now."

Chapter 18

DR SELFISH

Anna tried to keep track of the days by making daily marks on a wall by her bed. She had just drawn her sixth mark and was waiting for Wilson or some other guard to take her to the midday meal when someone new turned off her electronic barrier and entered. This young Tribani male was not wearing the usual silver uniform, but a subtle green outfit and dark shoes. He was not armed, so clearly, he was not a member of the security service. He was also wearing a nametag and holding an electronic tablet. He glanced at it and greeted her.

"Hello, Ana, my name is very selfish. I am the site's assistant medical leader. I'm here at the request of Captain Morrison to see if you have any medical issues or concerns, while you wait for his return."

Ana laughed and glanced at his nametag. It was written in the strange Kanji type characters she had seen everywhere, but the English version was written in very small letters below. His name was actually Barry Sailfish, which wasn't much better than his pronunciation.

"I'm just extremely bored. I don't think you can help with that."

He shook his head and then glanced at his tablet. "I have also been instructed to escort you to the dining hall for the midday meal. Perhaps we can talk more there."

"Of course."

There were generally no major distinguishing facial features among the Tribani males but at least this one had yellow hair and actually looked a lot like Lieutenant Long. She noticed he was smiling at her, which not many Tribanis did.

While they were eating, Ana decided to try a different subject for a non-security male.

"Are there special schools for medical persons?"

"Yes, of course. Some Earth years of schooling and more Earth years of practical training."

"Do you have a specific area of medicine?"

"General medicine." He laughed. "Of course, there was no preparation for human issues, since we had not seen any."

Ana noticed that, like Wilson, he seemed to take frequent glances at her chest.

"To change the subject, are you in a long-term relationship?"

He laughed. "Medical school didn't leave a lot of time for personal relationships."

He surprised her when he asked, "are you?"

"I had a boyfriend before I came here, but no long-term arrangement, like a marriage."

He frowned. "Marriage? Is that different than an agreement to stay with only one person?"

"Yes, there are civil ceremonies, but that is primarily a legal arrangement. A marriage is also a legal arrangement, but there are usually spiritual or religious aspects as well."

Barry seemed totally confused, so she decided to change the subject. "One of my guards couldn't describe any activities when Tribanis are not at work. What do you do when you are not working?"

He seemed confused. "Rest?"

"No hobbies…sports…games?"

He looked totally confused and shook his head "I'm not sure what you mean."

His tablet made a chiming noise, and he looked up at her. "I need to escort you back to your room."

On the way back to her room, Ana commented. "By the way, you last name is very unusual."

"Unusual?"

"A long time ago on Earth, family names, or last names, used to be given by the trade or occupation the person or family worked in, like baker, for example."

"Baker?"

"Someone that makes food from grains, like baking bread."

"Bread?"

She tried to describe bread, but he just shook his head, so she continued. "I've never heard of someone with the last name of a fish, like Sailfish."

"I don't know the origin of the name. I think many human names were assigned many generations ago."

As she entered her room, he commented. "I would like to give you an examination – to improve our knowledge of humans."

She thought to herself, '*I bet you would.*'

"Is this an order, or your idea?"

He seemed embarrassed. "My idea."

"I would agree if I can examine you."

He stared, obviously surprised. "Do you have medical training as well?"

"No, my exam would be on a purely physical level."

He stared at her for a moment then laughed, activated the door barrier, and left.

Chapter 19

CLOTHING TRIP

Ana had been a captive for a week. Her regular guards continued to escort her to the dining hall for the mostly tasteless meals three times a day and she was suffering from an extreme case of boredom. At least Lieutenant Long stopped by daily to see how she was doing. Ana was now familiar with the Tribani equivalent of a shower and toilet and machines that cleaned clothing, but she was tired of wearing the same clothes every day. Long had tried to find her some female Tribani clothing but they couldn't find a size that fit her body. Ana had an hourglass figure and virtually all the Tribani women were tall and slender. Lieutenant Long finally informed her she had permission to get some more clothes and Ana identified the clothing store on an aerial map.

Despite Ana's objections, her guards put her in handcuffs again and they entered a small ship for the short trip to the shopping center she was familiar with. She again asked Long to remove the handcuffs.

"These hurt. Please take them off. I won't try to escape."

"Sorry, but these are Captain Morrison's orders."

"We will only have 15 to 20 minutes before the resistance shows up."

"Then you must be fast and efficient in this hunt for new clothing."

Ana smiled at her comment, as Long had probably never been clothing shopping before. A few minutes later, the ship landed in front of Ana's familiar clothing store. Long took off the handcuffs and Ana opened the combination lock on the door and entered. Her two guards took up sentry duty at the door while Long followed her to the back of the store. Ana had been tired of carrying flashlights around, so she left one in each store she and Sam had visited. Long watched her crank the flashlight and followed her to the storage room in the back. Ana knew where everything she needed was and quickly started filling up a large cloth shoulder bag she took from a rack near the front of the store. Long followed her to the fitting room.

Ana flashed her light on the sign. "I would rather be alone to change clothes."

Long nodded and took up a sentry type position near the fitting rooms. A few minutes later Ana came out with a stylish new outfit on. Long stared at her.

"That is very different."

"Women here used to have many outfits, and all were different."

Long knew she was referring to the clothing the Tribani security females wore, which was basically all alike, with only minor variations in color and insignia.

Ana locked the door and they hurried to the ship. It took off in a matter of minutes – just as the resistance arrived too late to do anything.

Arun commented "they seem to be learning our tactics. I wonder what they wanted in a clothing store?"

Chapter 20

DAILY ROUTINE

The day after the clothing trip, Long received permission to take Ana on a trip to a grocery store to find some food she liked. She also wanted to retrieve some other "essentials", some makeup and even some perfume.

By this time, Morrison was no longer concerned about Ana trying to escape and a random guard would stop by early in the morning and unlock her door and she was pretty much free to roam the enormous ship by herself during the day, but not go outside. Most of the closed doors were not locked and she quickly found more comfortable sleeping quarters with a table and chairs. Most Tribanis did not live in the ship as they had moved out to the numerous small buildings surrounding the ship. Long told her the small buildings were transported in a "kit" form on the ship and constructed once they landed.

Long also approved her move to the larger and more comfortable sleeping room. She only had to stay in the room at night (with the door locked). Ana wondered how this room compared to the room Long lived in and asked her.

"It's not all that different. Would you like to see it?"

"Of course."

Long led Ana to her sleeping quarters. The room was a little larger than Ana's current quarters but much more efficient. At first there didn't appear to be any furniture, just walls with knobs. Long showed

Ana how her small bed folded down from the wall, as did other furniture in the room (a table with chairs and even a small sofa). The closet was a little larger, but the bathroom was the same as Ana's room.

"Are there any married couples in the security system?"

"Married?"

"Two people who are committed solely to the other in a formal relationship."

"We don't have exactly that, but we do have permanent relationships. They may or may not live together."

"If they did, it would be hard for two people to sleep in that bed."

"Why would they want to sleep in the same bed?"

Ana struggled to find a way to answer that. "Sometimes they may want to do it."

"Do what?"

"Have sex, procreate, whatever you call it." She suddenly remembered hearing the Tribani word for sex and said "khuis".

Long look shocked. "In their sleeping room? No, there are approved places for that."

Ana laughed at the thought of going to an approved place to have sex. "Are you in a permanent relationship?"

"No. It's hard to find this type of relationship when you are almost always on duty for security reasons."

"It's always hard to find the right person."

Long nodded then opened the door to escort Ana back to her room.

Ana extended her walks around the huge ship each day when she noticed her pants seemed to be getting tighter. The food was almost tasteless, but she found herself eating a lot more than she probably should. As she wandered around the ship, Ana noticed there were only a few doors that appeared to be locked (the lock on her own door was a different color when it was locked), and only a very few that were guarded. One day, she found her former escort Arthur Wilson guarding a door and stopped to chat with him. She noticed he sometimes stared at her chest and wondered what he was thinking. She still had never seen any public signs of affection among the Tribanis, no hugging or kissing or even hand holding. She wondered if it was forbidden in public or just a cultural norm.

While they were chatting, she had to move out of the way to let a transport vessel pulling several large carts loaded with yellow Madjuul plants pass in front. She was standing very close to Wilson, and she noticed him staring straight ahead, almost as if he were in a trance. She even passed her hand in front of his face, and he didn't respond. He seemed to regain his senses once she backed away from him. The next day, while they were chatting, she made a point of standing close to him and found the same result. She had read several medical books and knew about human pheromones and wondered if her pheromones were causing that response.

The following day, during her daily walk, she noticed a different sentry guarding the door press something on a small silver tube hanging from his belt to let someone in the door. Ana began chatting with the new guard, gradually moving closer to him until he was staring straight ahead. She examined the silver tube and pressed something that looked like a button. The door opened, and she quickly stepped inside. The room was full of electronic equipment she guessed to be communications and possibly computers. She quickly closed the door and stood near him as he recovered. She smiled at him when he recovered and looked at her. Why would they need to guard communications or computer equipment? Who were they guarding if from? She was the only human on board the enormous ship.

Maybe she could use the pheromone effect to help her in the future?

On the tenth day waiting for Captain Morrison's return, Barry Sailfish stopped by to check on her again.

He didn't mention the examination, so Ana reminded him of her offer.

"Have you thought any more about your medical examination and my physical examination?"

He laughed. "I have…a lot."

"And?"

"Without prior approval, I could suffer a type of discipline, that would make my work here difficult."

"What if we didn't tell anyone?"

"Unapproved actions are extremely difficult to keep secret. As much as the idea appeals, even…" He struggled for the right word. Ana suggested "excites".

He laughed. "Yes, but I need to seek approval first."

Ana suddenly remembered the pheromone issue and slowly started walking closer to him. He didn't even realize it until his eyes glazed over.

He was a little bit taller than her, but she put her arms around him and kissed him. She laughed and started her own physical examination with her hands. When she finished, she sat back down on her bed and waited. A few minutes later he looked at her.

"What just happened?"

"What do you mean?"

"What were we talking about?"

"You were talking about receiving approval for a medical examination to further your knowledge of humans."

He laughed. "Oh, yes. Well, I will let you know if I receive approval."

He left Ana thinking about her own examination that confirmed her suspicions that her pheromones led to arousals as well as trance-like states.

Finally, after two weeks, Captain Morrison returned with good news and met her in the conference room. He immediately noticed her new clothes and makeup. Morrison wasn't all that physically different from the other security service males she had met, but the more she associated with the Tribanis, the more their different personalities became evident. She even wondered what he was like on a personal basis. He seemed concerned for her comfort and wellbeing, even asking about her daily routine. Then he turned to conversation to her idea of a peace agreement.

"The prince and his Advisory Council have agreed to your idea of a peace agreement. They have asked us to help you convince the groups attacking us to make such an agreement."

Ana was curious. "Has any other human contact suggested a peace agreement?"

"No, only you. Everyone else seems determined to try and make us go back to Tribanus."

Ana couldn't help but notice Morrison was staring at her. She had some ideas other than peace treaties she wanted to discuss with him. But first she needed to clarify his comment. "Prince?"

"Soon I will try to explain our organization – our government to you."

"Why not now? Maybe it will help in my negotiations if I understand how you are organized and governed."

Morrison glanced at a status monitor. The screen was filled with characters not all that different from Japanese Kanji characters. "Not today, but we can hold this discussion tomorrow. I have asked an expert in our history to help you understand our history and how we came to be here. He should arrive tomorrow."

Chapter 21

HISTORY LESSON

The only Tribani historian on Earth entered the ship's officer's planning room to find Captain John Morrison and a young human woman waiting at a table. He had been briefed about the purpose of the meeting and brought some historical data and images on an electronic storage device. He had never seen a human woman like Ana and was surprised at her looks. He had seen a few human females that had been captured near the London encampment and assumed human women would be all the same as were his own species, even down to the clothing they wore. Ana was wearing a colorful red blouse and blue jeans and he immediately noticed her long curly black hair and large dark eyes and something he had never seen before – makeup. Her lips were bright red. Even her fingernails were red. He couldn't help but notice her hourglass figure either and stared at her. For her part, this alien looked like all the others.

Morrison had to get his attention. "Robert, we are here to provide a background to Ana to help her understand our situation and how we came to be here, so she can help us find a way to work together to avoid unnecessary violence and deaths."

Robert quickly regained his composure and pressed some storage device buttons wirelessly connecting his personal storage device to the room's display system.

"Hello, my English name is Robert Mayfield. I think I'm the only Remembrance Official or what you would call a historian that traveled to Earth. First if you have any questions, please ask them. I want to help Captain Morrison in his task to help you understand why we are here, so let me begin. Since we are on Earth, I will use the term years to describe the time frame and the numbering system based on the powers of ten."

"Slightly more than 2000 years ago, our scientists determined that our sun was burning out and to survive as a species, we would have to migrate to another solar system. Fortunately, we had just discovered what you would call a space drive system that enabled teams of searchers to try and find alternative planets. We searched all over this part of the galaxy and found very few suitable planets that were habitable. Only one had significant quantities of water and enough farmable land needed for our survival – Earth."

Ana was sitting with her arms folded and listening carefully. "In your search did you encounter any other intelligent species?"

"Yes, there are numerous other species with similar or even more advanced technology. There are certain areas of the galaxy where we frequently encountered others. Earth happens to be in a relatively remote area so not many other species have visited. The Tribani ship that discovered Earth also encountered another species that had chosen Earth for an outpost where they could resupply before continuing their future raids on inhabitable worlds and warned us to stay away. They were a warlike species not all that different than what humans call pirates. This conflict escalated and eventually led to a protracted war that left both sides' war making capabilities depleted. We finally convinced them migration to Earth was a matter of survival for us, so they appeared to abandon their plan for the utilization of Earth as a re-supply outpost and returned to their home planet. That was fortunate as there weren't many Tribani warriors left. We found out later that they had not abandoned those plans, only changed them."

Ana didn't comment, so Robert continued.

"The first Tribani ship that visited Earth made several aerial surveys during the day and at night. Most of what you know as Europe was relatively uninhabited, so they landed in one of the more populated areas – the country of England. Based on their surveys, they estimated the population of Earth at that time to be about 250 million. From books and documents they brought back, this was the year England identified as 1005. The survey team members were careful to stay hidden as they surveyed several towns and collected plants, human blood and animal samples and artifacts such as books and recorded many visual images and sounds. Unfortunately, despite extensive efforts to avoid breathing unfiltered air or drinking unfiltered water, on the way back all the survey team died as they had somehow contracted micro-organisms from the air or the water. Fortunately, the survey team had been isolated from the rest of the ship's crew and they returned safely."

Ana wondered why they knew English. This helped explain the origin. In her weeks of captivity, it seemed that some Tribani would only speak their native language while others tried to make conversations with her to improve their English fluency.

"Why do so few Tribanis try to speak English?"

"Most Tribanis can read and write some English, but we had only a few ancient recordings of people speaking English before we landed on Earth, and some base camps have reported encountering humans that are speaking other languages."

"Where did you learn to speak English so fluently?"

"I live in the London encampment. Some humans near the camp tried to attack us and we captured some. I have spent quite some time with some of them, just to learn how English is spoken. As you know, speaking English is a requirement for those in the security service."

When Ana nodded, Robert continued his history lesson.

"When the survivors of the first survey reported back, the news impacted all of our society. Our doctors and scientists studied the dead and surviving crew members and some human and animal blood samples they had collected along with plant, soil and water samples and concluded that to survive on Earth we would have start a process to change our DNA to be more like humans. This was explained to be a slow painful process that would take at least fifty to sixty generations, or more than 1000 years.

She wondered what the unchanged Tribani looked like. Maybe it was better that she didn't know – at least for now.

"At that point, each person or family had to decide whether they wanted to migrate or not. If they did, then they would have to begin the process that would affect them and their children and their children's children. Basically, society broke into two camps, those leaving and those staying. For simplicity, I will refer to them as "leavers" and "stayers".

"The leavers began studying English history and the structure of the language and decided to adopt a similar form of monarchy type government in the belief they would better be able to blend in. After some internal strife and near warfare, a king emerged among the leavers. Our current king is his direct descendent."

"What form of government existed prior to the discovery of Earth?"

Robert thought about that for a moment. "To use an analogy, it was not all that different from the organization of bees in a beehive. Like the queen, we had a strong central leader with a small favored or royal group, a small group of scientists and engineers, a worker bee group, and a security group – to protect the hive. Making the change to a monarchy type government was relatively easy."

Ana laughed, as that was fairly descriptive. She didn't say anything, so Robert continued.

"While the DNA transformation was underway, one of the first king's descendants decided to send another survey party to Earth to see if anything had changed. That team arrived around the year 1500. Based on new aerial surveys, they determined the population of Earth had already doubled to an estimated 500 million, which was very concerning. How would we be able to blend in after 500 more years, if there were already a huge number of humans on Earth and virtually no area that was not already occupied?"

Robert tapped his tablet to display several aerial night views of Earth from the 2nd survey. There were many lights in England and parts of Europe.

"By that time, the leavers were far into the DNA conversion and life on our own planet was becoming extremely difficult due to the DNA change. Our sun was also continuing to expand, heating the planet even more and making it difficult for anyone to survive outside of enclosed cities. Eventually, there were separate cities for the leavers and the stayers as their foods and biological systems, and even the air they breathed became incompatible. As a result, the leavers collectively decided they had no option at that point but to migrate despite the number of humans they would face."

"Another descendent of the first king decided to send one final survey to Earth. They arrived in the year 1895 and based on their aerial surveys found the population of Earth since the last survey had again tripled to more than fifteen hundred million. Based on some forward-looking projections, that meant there could be more than seven thousand million humans on Earth when we finally migrated."

A graph was displayed that projected human populations until the end of the 21st century, when more than twelve thousand million humans could be living on Earth.

"In the assessment that followed, it appeared that human technology had also advanced significantly, especially in the ability to conduct warfare and it seemed likely humans on an already heavily populated world, would not let us migrate without a major fight. And with seven thousand million enemies, we probably would not survive, even with a technological advantage."

"The original plan would no longer work so many alternatives were discussed. These alternatives even included living in domed cities under the sea."

Robert laughed at the thought of living under the sea. Ana and Morrison didn't respond, so he continued.

"The most likely chance of success was determined to be the establishment of 1000 small encampments or villages of 1000 inhabitants each in as many remote and uninhabited places as could be identified. Based on the latest medical and scientific projections, our DNA would not be completely compatible with humans for another 8-9 generations."

"While this was going on, the pirate-like species, the Romanis, occasionally visited our planet secretly and each time when they were discovered, they were driven off. What we didn't know was some of the Tribani stayers had been contacted by the Romanis and some became spies for them."

"The Tribani stayers had finally realized they could no longer stay on Tribanis as the sun continued to expand and heat the surface much faster than the scientists has predicted and so they contacted the Romanis to find them a new world where they could exist without changing their DNA. In exchange they would run that world as an outpost for the Romanis, supplying them with suitable food and water."

"When we found out about this, we decided to infiltrate that spy network to discover their full plans. Our spy immediately learned the Romanis had not abandoned their plans for Earth as it was still a better choice than the planet selected for the stayers.

"Their spies had told them about the changes in population of Earth and its advances in science and military weapons, and they concluded they could not defeat Earth either, so they had to find another way to get rid of the human threat. That's when they came up with the idea of a chemical attack that would slowly eliminate the humans without destroying the Earth and its resources that they needed."

Ana wondered if this were true or just something they made up to make it look like they weren't behind the attack. "How long have you known about the chemical attack plan?"

"We knew about the plan, but not the method they planned to introduce the chemical, or when they would execute the plan. We only found out about that after it had happened. Our spy reported the details as soon as the Romanis told the stayers."

Morrison could sense that Ana was having a hard time believing the story as Robert was describing it.

"Ana, this was a big problem for us as well. When we found out about the meteor shower, we still were 3-4 generations away from the required DNA conversion and our scientists determined this chemical would have an even greater effect on us than humans."

Ana frowned. "How did you learn the nature of the chemical that was being used?"

"It was in the plans our spy intercepted from the Romanis. By the way, our scientists determined this chemical would have virtually no effect on the stayers but an even bigger effect on the Romanis who came to Earth after the chemical has been dispersed."

"So why not just wait until the chemical biologically degrades, and then migrate?"

"We would have, but the spy networks were exposed somehow, perhaps by the Romanis just to cause problems. This information led to a major civil war between the leavers and the stayers. The stayers greatly outnumbered the leavers and some of our transports were destroyed before our King made a hasty decision to leave before the DNA transformation was complete."

"Although some 15 years had passed since the meteor shower, the same effects were experienced by our people as humans who were exposed initially – as we were more susceptible. Even now, a number of our people in each encampment have experienced severe memory losses."

Ana was still skeptical. "How do I know that you are not making all of this up, and the meteor shower was actually your doing?"

Morrison volunteered to provide proof "I could let you observe some of our people who have been affected in this encampment, if that would help convince you."

Robert noticed Ana seemed to be thinking about that offer, so he continued with his history lesson.

"No plan is perfect, of course, and the Romanis didn't know that some percentage of humans would be immune to the chemical. Our initial assessment is that one to three percent of humans were unaffected and that probably means there are still between seventy and two hundred million humans on Earth today. We took every precaution we could to avoid contact with whatever is left of the chemical but some of our people were nevertheless affected, as you could see, if you want to."

He paused as Ana was staring at him, deep in thought. "How many Tribanis migrated?"

"Approximately one million in one hundred ships with an average of ten thousand migrants each. Some ships are larger than this one, some are smaller."

"Did all the leavers leave Tribanus?"

"Not all. There were several thousand potential leavers who decided they really didn't want to leave even though the sun was making Tribanus unlivable."

"Ok, where is your current king?"

"He decided to establish his base camp near the city of London."

Ana pushed her chair back from the table. "Now that you've told me all this, and you have discussed my initial offer with your leaders, what is it that you want me to do?"

Morrison replied "Our camps, and our people, have been attacked at many of the base camps we have established. There have been no other communications with any human group seeking a peaceful solution to our migration. We can't return to our home planet due to its extreme environment and our incompatibility with it now that our DNA is almost human."

Ana remembered Arun's claim that the Baytown group had tried to negotiate. "We heard another group near here tried to negotiate some type of agreement and were laughed out of the room."

Morrison seemed shocked. "I can assure you; no one else has asked about negotiating but you. I oversee the overall security for this site, and several other sites near here, and I would have been involved in any such discussions. So, we hope you will try and understand what happened and why we would like you to work with us to find a compromise of some sort that could lead to a peaceful resolution for everyone. We are experiencing increasingly violent attacks on our encampments at other locations and there are some among us that want to fight back and wipe out any humans that attack us. I don't think that's what you want either."

"Of course not! So where do we start?"

"We think you should meet first with your own group and if that is successful, meet with other groups that are near here. Then, if that proves successful, we will bring you to other parts of this continent to explain the agreement to other groups."

"What are you prepared to offer?"

"You mentioned restoring the electrical system. We developed a process I think you would call nuclear fusion. We could connect several fusion reactors into the old power system at former power plants. We could also restart the water treatment plants. I understand in talking to Lieutenant Long, clean water appears to be in short supply. After that, there could be other areas where we could provide assistance."

Ana knew that re-establishing power and clean water would be an immense help. If they could somehow get the refineries back in operation, they would be able to get trucks and even cars going again. The alternatives to a peace agreement would be horrific.

"What happens if a resistance group does not agree to a peace agreement?"

"We hope that will not happen, but we will address it then."

"OK, when can we start?"

"Immediately."

"I need to send a message to Arun Patel, my group's military leader about a meeting to talk about a peace agreement."

"How do you want to do that?"

"They need to know it's from me, so they will agree to a meeting."

"Tell us what you need."

"I will, but first I would like to see the Tribanis that were affected by the meteor's chemical."

Morrison opened the door for her. "This way."

Ana could sense that no one wanted to talk about the Tribanis affected by the chemical as they were kept in a separate small domed area. Several caretakers were trying to assist a few dozen Tribanis who appeared to have a hard time eating, speaking or even dressing. These were the same effects she was very familiar with from taking care of her own parents. When Ana looked closer, she could see more physical effects such as the inability by some to use their arms or legs. Some had large lumps and red patches on their skin. There were other issues she wouldn't even be able to discuss with her own team members. She signaled to Morrison she was ready to leave.

Chapter 22

NEGOTIATIONS BEGIN

Early the next morning, Arun found a small package sitting on top of the hood of the flatbed truck. He opened it and found a note wrapped around a tube of lipstick that summarized Ana's hope for a peace agreement and the need for negotiations. He was relieved that she was still alive but after his brief time in captivity, he tended to agree with Ana that defeating the Tribanis, or even causing them enough problems that they would want to leave, was not feasible. So, her request to meet to discuss an agreement really didn't surprise him. Later that day, he and Sam drove to the electronic fence where a guard was waiting to accept his reply as to the time and location of the meeting.

The Tribanis (really Captain Morrison) didn't want anything to happen to Ana, so Lieutenant Long and several guards attended the meeting with Sam and Arun and a few other resistance members at their warehouse. This was the first time the rest of the members of the resistance had seen aliens. Arun was surprised how Ana's appearance seemed to improve every time he saw her. She had been gone for less than a month and he realized he missed her.

Arun did recognize Lieutenant Long from his interrogations after the mortar attack, and he was wondering what she was like when she wasn't wearing her security uniform. Every time Lieutenant Long looked at Arun, he smiled at her. After a while she instinctively smiled back. She also wondered about Arun after her initial encounter with him as his interrogator.

Ironically, Ana and Sam met at the start of negotiations. It was rather awkward as Sam knew she now held an important role in the negotiations with the aliens. Was she really trying to make the best of the situation, or was she secretly a traitor? He hoped it was the former.

After some time passed, Sam had assumed he would never see her again and had found a new girlfriend, the daughter of another resistance member. Sheena was shorter than Ana, with red hair and green eyes. Sam motioned her to come over.

"Sheena, I want you to meet Ana. She will be a liaison between us and the aliens to help find a peaceful solution."

Sheena walked over, put her arms around Sam and kissed him, ignoring Ana. "You think too much." She laughed and started to "skip" away. Sam called to her, "Don't you want to meet Ana?"

She stopped, looked back, laughed, then continued skipping away.

Ana stared after her. "She seems kind of dumb."

"She's not a genius like you but she's okay."

"I'm not a genius, I just read a lot." She looked away at Sheena. "She's probably so affectionate you don't notice."

Sam laughed.

Ana began with a high-level summary of the "history" lesson she had with Robert Morrison and described the dozens of Tribanis affected by the chemical. There was a lot of skepticism and disbelief at first that the Tribanis had not been behind the meteor shower that had wreaked so much death and suffering on Earth. After a brief discussion, Arun asked the negotiators to get back to the subject of a peace treaty.

In effect, the negotiations were mostly one way as the resistance group really couldn't offer much to the Tribanis other than they would stop trying to attack them. They really wanted the power restored. It didn't take long to finalize an agreement in writing and Ana returned to Captain Morrison with the agreement. He was pleased at the agreement, but more pleased that nothing happened to her, and she was back – with some interesting new clothes and different makeup.

While she was with Sam and Arun, she contacted the Baytown group about a meeting to discuss a peace type agreement. They were not thrilled at first but agreed to meet her. She also asked Arun if she could take a chess set with her as she was often bored waiting for decisions to be made. Arun happily gave her two sets and said he regretted they had not had time to set up a chess tournament in the camp.

Ana then discussed the need to take some pictures of the suffering Tribanis as evidence of the effect of the chemical on them, and Arun provided her with his working solar-powered camera. Taking pictures of the suffering Tribanis was somewhat emotional for Ana, but she managed to get what she thought she needed as proof. Captain Morrison had again escorted her to the affected Tribanis and watched her taking pictures with Arun's camera.

"What are you doing, Ana?"

"I will need proof that Tribanis are affected when we discuss the peace agreement with the Baytown group, and other resistance groups as well. My group believed me, but others may not."

Morrison motioned her to give him the camera and he examined it carefully before giving it back to her. "Can you show me?"

Ana showed him some of the pictures she had taken before he interrupted her. "Why don't you just use the picture function of a tablet?"

"I don't have one."

Morrison then used his tablet, took her picture, and showed it to her.

She nodded. "That's even better than Arun's camera."

"I will issue you a tablet." He then motioned Ana to follow him and headed for the exit door. As she followed him, she wondered what else she would find on one of the tablets that all security personnel carried.

As soon as Morrison gave her a new security tablet, she found a system for communicating by text messages. She used a search function to find the name of a communications specialist and asked him how to transfer the pictures in Arun's camera to her tablet. When that was completed, she gave Arun's camera to Long and asked if she would return it to him for her. Long agreed and made plans to visit Arun AND return the camera.

Captain Morrison didn't want to take any chances that something might happen to Ana, so this time he transported several representatives of the Baytown group to the main ship for the negotiations. Lieutenant Long was there for the Tribanis in case some new requests or requirements were raised during the negotiations and Captain Morrison attended at the beginning just to emphasize their desire to reach an agreement.

Ana had communicated with the Baytown group in the past but never actually met them. It was a little awkward at first, but after Ana provided the same high-level summary concerning the meteor shower and showed them some pictures of the affected Tribanis on her new tablet, they eventually agreed to almost the same terms as her own group.

At the end of the negotiations Ana pulled John Ryder, the leader of the Baytown resistance, aside and asked if they had ever attacked the Tribanis.

"We never saw any sentries, but one time a few of them wandered outside the perimeter fence to look at the nearby plants and animals and one of our guys shot one of them. The rest ran inside and soon we were attacked by a small ship with some kind of heat ray weapon. We lost two fighters and decided to wait until we had some more powerful weapons before we confronted them again."

"Why not try to contact them to discuss a possible peace agreement?"

Ryder seemed surprised at the question. "Why would we do that? We just want them gone. I was really surprised when you contacted me about a peace agreement. I was skeptical to say the least, but willing to listen. After what I heard today, I'm somewhat hopeful we can make this work."

Ana smiled at the partially true story that they had never tried to contact the Tribanis about a treaty, but subsequently attacked them when they happened to wander outside their encampment. They had not contacted them first.

Neither Ana nor Ryder were aware of yet another resistance group to the south of the Tribani encampment as they had made no contact with any other resistance group and had no interaction with the Tribanis.

A New Resistance

Morrison was greatly relieved and informed the base inhabitants that the attacks should stop, and they were free to leave the base if they needed to, but they should still use caution around humans.

Others in the encampment didn't like the time the captain was spending with Ana while trying to work out arrangements at other base camps for a peace agreement. They suspected the captain was becoming involved with her.

They did spend a lot of time talking and planning future negotiations. Morrison knew that Ana was tired of being confined to the spaceship, so he started escorting her on long walks around the encampment.

She was curious and took the opportunity to ask if he was in a permanent relationship.

"No. My duties keep me very busy. I really don't have the time for that."

That answer was not all that different from Lieutenant Long's reason, and she was surprised when John asked her a similar question.

"Were you in a permanent relationship with someone in your resistance group?"

"Not really. I had a boyfriend, which is not exactly the same. When we started the negotiations with them, I saw him. I had been away for a while and he probably thought I was never coming back, so he found someone else to live with."

"That must have been…difficult."

Ana agreed it was and they dropped the subject. She was wondering about the slow DNA conversion process and asked him. "How do you slowly modify your DNA to become more like humans?"

He seemed reluctant to reply but simply said "it's a series of injections. One every 10 Earth days or so, all year long, every year."

She winced at the thought of that. "Sounds painful."

"Not too painful. There is a pressurized injector, and the liquid is absorbed quickly through the skin."

"And you've been doing this all your life?"

He nodded. "We start once we learn to walk, and it continues until we die. If we had not done this, we probably would not have survived on Tribanus for very long as the scientists were slowly changing the air and water there to be more compatible with Earth. We certainly would not have survived for the very long here once we left the ships that brought us."

"And this has been going on for more than a thousand years?"

"Yes. There was no alternative."

Ana just shook her head at the thought of injections, painful or not, with no end.

A small open cart passed them, and Ana wondered if Morrison might know more about them than Private Wilson.

"What kind of power do those small carts use?"

"I'm not sure but I think water is somehow converted to its basic elements and then those gases are combined and burned to power the cart and recharge the water convertor. After some use, the cart's primary energy source must be re-charged, and the water tank re-filled."

Ana thought about that for a moment. Wilson was right in a way, as the carts did run on water. If she didn't need to walk a lot to keep from gaining weight, she might have asked Morrison to let her borrow one. She would like to see the whole encampment, but she wasn't sure if they would let her do that yet. Maybe in time…

The next day on their evening walk they were attacked by the local resistance group just south of the encampment. The best the group had come up with were homemade pipe bombs and when they spotted Ana and Captain Morrison through the fence walking toward them, they tossed one over the fence at Morrison. Their aim was poor, but it exploded close enough to them to knock them both down. As the dust cleared, Morrison saw Ana struggling to get up. He yelled at her.

"Are you all right, Ana?"

"Yes, go get those idiots."

Morrison used a small communicator to alert his team and immediately two scout ships began searching the area just outside the fence. They employed multiple forms of surveillance technology and quickly found two resistance members running away from the encampment.

When they were spotted, they fired a crude mortar shell at the spacecraft - which caused no damage. Morrison ordered a modified version of the meteor chemical that would only knock them out, used on them, and the scout team brought the two back to the base as captives. Ana was a little shaken but suffered no injuries and waved off Morrison's offer to take her to the ship's hospital.

When the captives were awake, Long took Ana to meet them. Morrison had converted two sleeping quarters into holding cells, like Ana's first holding cell.

One of the resistance members was sitting on a bunk, seemingly not interested in discussing anything but the other was standing with his arms folded, staring out the door. Both captives were shocked to see a human so closely associated with the aliens and even more surprised at Ana's appearance. Their own group included a few women but they, like most human women of the day, wore fatigues and caps and were rather all alike. Ana surely stood out. They also noticed Long was carrying a weapon of some sort and knew that was to ensure they didn't try to attack them should they escape somehow from the holding cell. The member standing moved closer to the door and stared at Long and Ana. Ana noticed he was a little taller than Sam and about the same age, but he had something she had never seen before – Asian features.

"What's your name?"

"Kaito Tanaka." He smiled at her. "What's your name?"

"Ana Cordoba. Why did your group never try to contact any other resistance groups?"

"We are only a dozen and didn't have any resources to try and reach out to other groups. We have several really smart members, but no one with any practical knowledge on how to make things work without electricity."

Ana thought of Sam and smiled. "Okay, then why did you throw an explosive device at Captain Morrison and me?"

Ana laughed when he replied. "We just wanted to get your attention."

"For what purpose?" Ana realized she was repeating Morrison's initial questioning of her.

"We wanted to meet someone in charge to see if we could work together somehow."

"By attacking a civilian and a security official? Why not just talk to a sentry?"

"We've never seen one."

Morrison had seen Ana and Long outside the jail cell where the resistance members were being held and wandered over to see what the discussion was about. He overheard Kaito's comment about never seeing a sentry. He was immediately skeptical of that as to his knowledge; patrols of the perimeter were scheduled several times a day. He made a mental note to ask Long to follow up on that with the perimeter sentry team leader.

Ana and Long turned to Morrison when he commented. "Perhaps you should offer this group the same deal as we made with the other resistance groups? You don't have to stand here to do this. You can use the officer's conference room."

Long turned off the electronic barrier to Kaito's cell and waved him to follow Ana and they all left for the conference room. Long followed Kaito with her weapon ready, just in case.

After some discussions including Ana's now standard description of the nature of the meteor shower and its effects on Tribanis and humans, she described the deal offered to other groups, Kaito immediately agreed, subject to everyone else in his group also agreeing. He also said they were a stubborn group, and it could take some time to get them to agree to the proposal. Morrison released Kaito and his companion to discuss the proposal with his resistance group.

Chapter 23

MEDICAL SUPPLIES

Later that day, Morrison confided to her that their medical supplies were running low due to the unexpected and constant attacks at some base camps. She suggested they could gather what they needed from a large pharmacy that, unknown to them, happened to be located near the resistance group just south of the encampment. They landed at night to avoid an attack by possible resistance groups. Ana tried to warn them.

"Don't open the door with the lights on!"

Morrison understood her warning, but it was too late. A hail of gunfire came in the open door with bullets ricocheting around the room next to the open door. Morrison pulled Ana down and covered her body with his. He suddenly groaned and rolled off her. He had been hit in the shoulder by a ricocheting bullet. The door had been closed by now and Ana started examining the wound. John was bleeding a lot. She tried to stop the bleeding by pressing on the wound and yelled at the crew gathered around to get a doctor. One ran off to get him and in a few minutes the doctor returned with a stretcher, and they carried Morrison to a small emergency clinic in the ship. The doctor saw blood on her shirt and hands and asked if she was injured. Ana didn't even notice Morrison's blood on her. She shook her head, and the doctor asked her to wait where she was. Ana was worried about John but after a while fell asleep. She woke up when the doctor returned and told her she could see him.

Morrison was lying on a table with his shirt off with a huge bandage on one shoulder. The bullet must have gone through him. Ana hadn't seen John without a shirt – he was quite muscular. She walked to him and took his hand.

"You saved my life."

He smiled. "It is my duty."

The ship's captain entered to check on Morrison and told them they were returning to the base. Ana didn't want to give up on the hunt for medical supplies so over the objection of Morrison, she described the shopping center she was familiar with. She knew of a smaller pharmacy near there. The ship's captain led her to the bridge and together they conducted an aerial survey of the shopping center until Ana recognized the former pharmacy. Lieutenant Long led a team to scout the pharmacy. With Ana's help the team returned to the ship with a large cache of medical supplies.

The ship returned to the base and the next day while Ana was eating breakfast she was surprised when Morrison walked into the dining hall. She could see a large bandage under his uniform, but he seemed okay.

"John!" She jumped up and ran to him and hugged him. He had not been that close to her before. Her perfume and pheromones overwhelmed him, and he stared off into space. When he didn't respond to her hug she let go and saw him seemingly in a trance.

"John?"

Now that she was back a bit, he recovered his senses and looked at her. "Yes?"

"Are you okay?"

"Yes." He frowned. "What just happened?"

Ana remembered the medical books she had read and her interaction with her own guard and the electronics room guard and Barry Sailfish and guessed what happened. She hugged him again to be sure (she was just gathering some data). He was overwhelmed again. She stepped back, saw him, and laughed. Just to gather more data, she put her arms around him and kissed him. He almost blacked out. She saw him lost in a deep trance. She didn't know that Tribanis don't kiss at all and rarely embraced except on special occasions.

She pulled a chair near him and sat down watching him. He finally recovered and looked at her.

"I don't think you'd survive, if we actually did it."

He didn't understand. "What are you talking about?"

"You seem to go into a trance whenever I'm close to you."

He just stared at her. She needed to find out if it was her pheromones or her perfume. She asked him to rest a bit while she cleaned up. She took a shower, dressed and found John in the ship's officer's conference room trying to read an English book. He saw her and stood up. She walked to him, put her arms around him and kissed him again. This time he slowly hugged her until he went into a trance-like state. Her pheromones were strong, but he could survive them for a brief period if they weren't combined with her perfume. That test had her wondering how she could take things to the next level. She had been pretty lonely for the last few months, and this was taking her mind off her captivity and the work on the peace agreements.

When he recovered, Ana asked John why she never saw public displays of affection or even couples holding hands. John replied that it was cultural. Sex was only for procreation. She told him they were missing a lot. After meeting her, he agreed.

She was tired of the sterile atmosphere of the spaceship and asked John if they could go for another evening walk around the encampment. John agreed and after walking around and some small chat, Ana took his hand while they strolled around. He didn't seem to mind. They stopped to look at the sunset and happened to look at each other. Ana put her arms around him and kissed him. He kissed her back and she was surprised when his hands wandered to her breasts until he was overcome and stood staring off into space. She waited for him to regain his senses.

"Ever wonder what it's like to do it for fun instead of procreation?"

"I try not to think about that. It just makes me frustrated."

"Maybe I can help with that." She kissed him and put her hand on his crotch confirming what she already knew. When he recovered and looked at her, she asked "Do you know where we can be alone for a while?"

He laughed but he was thinking about it. "There is a storage area near here..."

"Show me."

He led her to a remote storage facility still within the compound. It was piled high with goods that were transported and there was some packing material in a pile near the door. Ana felt the material. "This is soft enough."

He laughed but stopped when she took off her blouse. "Ana?"

She walked to him and opened his shirt's snaps and started running her fingers around his chest. He was almost in a trance again and she backed off, so he could regain his senses.

"It's too bad you won't remember most of this."

He was mesmerized when she took off her bra and jeans. "Well? What are you waiting for?"

He managed to get most of his clothes off before she pushed him, and he fell on the pile of packing material, then jumped on him.

When he came to his senses Anna was dressed and sitting on a metal box. "I thought you would get in trouble if I just left."

He dressed quickly, trying to remember what happened. As they were walking back to the transport, he had to ask. "What just happened?"

"We did it. Or, rather, I did it with you. It was pretty good for me."

"What did we do?"

"We did it."

"Did what?"

"Fooled around, had sex, or 'khuis.'"

He stopped and stared at her. "No. It's not possible."

She stopped and turned to him. "Why not?"

"I would remember."

"Obviously, you don't."

He stared at her for a moment. "You can't imagine how much I wish I could remember what happened. "

She laughed and started walking toward the main ship. "You will next time. We'll figure it out."

He started following her, shaking his head.

The next day she had a confidential discussion with the site's lead doctor Hugh Grant, and asked if he could think of a way for John to not lose his senses because of her pheromones.

Grant was having his own problem as she was near him. He had never been that close to her before. He started to feel dizzy and realized the problem. He promised he would get back to her with a possible solution.

The next day, John proudly showed her two tiny cylinders in his hand.

"What are those?"

"A kind of filter that goes into the nose. Dr Grant said the filter material should stop most of your emissions that are causing me to lose consciousness."

She laughed. "Want to try it tonight?"

John's hormonal response was immediate. "Oh, yes!"

Later that evening they returned to the storage facility and this time John was almost unaffected by her pheromones. It was totally different when he was responding to her. An hour later, she was exhausted, and John was still going strong.

The next day, Ana was wondering if her pheromones would affect a female Tribani. She found Lieutenant Long seated at a desk, entering a daily log in a tablet, and wandered over to stand right behind her. She pretended to be interested in the daily log, but she really wanted to see if her pheromones would affect Long. Long looked up at her, seemingly unaffected. "Can I help you, Ana?"

"No, I was just wondering what's in the daily log you keep."

"It's just a form that we used to record anything out of the ordinary." She handed her tablet to Ana to read. By this time, Ana had a basic reading knowledge of the Tribani language and read a pretty boring report on the day's activities from several security personnel. One perimeter guard noted a deer had died trying to run through the fence. Ana laughed.

"What is funny, Ana?"

"You probably have never eaten deer. It can be tasty."

"Tasty? You mean you eat these animals?" Long was shocked.

Ana remembered Private Wilson's reaction to the idea of eating animals, so she wasn't surprised. "Yes, but only after they've been properly prepared and cooked. It's only fair since some animals eat humans when they can."

Long stood up and ran to the nearest bathroom. When she returned, Ana commented. "Not all humans eat animals. Some eat only fruits and vegetables."

Long just shook her head. "I have never tried any human food that I liked."

"Maybe you will someday."

Ana said goodbye and returned to her sleeping quarters wondering why only Tribani males seemed to be affected by human female pheromones.

Chapter 24

GAMES

na was walking briskly around the ship in an attempt to keep from gaining more weight when she ran into Dr. Sailfish leaving a sleeping compartment. He seemed happy to see her.

"Hello Ana, how are you?"

He held his electronic tablet against his chest while closing the compartment door. The tablet had a medical report with the information displayed in a checkerboard pattern, and it reminded her of the chess and checker set Arun had given her.

"I didn't know there were games available on the tablets everyone carries about."

Sailfish glanced at the tablet. "Games? This is a medical report."

"Oh, are there games available on the tablets?"

"I'm not sure what you mean."

"I've asked several Tribanis what they do when they are not working, and they always say 'nothing' or 'rest' like you did. I was just wondering if anyone plays board games when they aren't working or maybe when they are bored like I am a lot. Or, if there are games available on the tablets if someone wanted to play."

"I'm not sure what a 'board game' is."

"Do you have a minute? I have one in my sleeping compartment. I could show you."

Sailfish looked at his tablet for a moment then nodded. He started following Ana to her compartment.

She retrieved the chess and checker set from her backpack and started to set it up on a small table near her bed while Sailfish watched. She set up the chess set first and started describing the moves each piece could make. After a few minutes, he interrupted her.

"That seems like a very complicated undertaking, that would take a long time to learn. I don't think I would have a chance to win such a game."

Ana thought about that. "You're right. It's rather complicated. What about checkers?"

She moved the chess pieces off the board, flipped it over and started putting checker pieces on the board. Sailfish's expression changed.

"That sort of looks like draeger."

Ana glanced up at him. "Draeger?"

"Yes. I have a draeger set. I can bring it and show it to you tomorrow."

"Sounds great."

The next day, Sailfish stopped by Ana's compartment and showed her what he called a board game. It was a flat piece of metal that unfolded several times until it was similar in size to Ana's checkers game. Instead of a square checkerboard pattern, the positions were all octagons with eight sides instead of four, and the overall board had eight sides with 10 positions on each side. He started placing 8-sided red pieces in a row down the middle of the board and blue pieces around the perimeter on one side of the board (40 total).

She noticed that the red pieces in the center were three times taller than the blue perimeter pieces.

Before he could start explaining the rules, Ana asked "why does everyone say they don't play games. It looks like you could play this when you are not working?"

Sailfish thought for a second. "Because we don't play other Tribanis, we play against a timer. The questions you have asked makes it sound like two players playing against each other."

He went on to explain the rules in which blue pieces are moved from the perimeter in a straight line to be next to a red pieces in the middle of the board. He further explained that you must take your hand off that piece to stack it on another piece of the same color. Blue pieces must occupy all the spaces next to the red pieces before they can be stacked. Blue pieces are then stacked until they are three in height and then a fourth blue piece can jump over the red center line pieces and continue to the opposite perimeter. The player moves as many pieces in straight lines as possible in the allotted time, then the timer is restarted, and the player must begin with another blue piece from the perimeter. The goal is to move all blue perimeter pieces from one side to the other side's perimeter in as few timing events as possible. There were 40 perimeter pieces to move, and the player could only use one hand at a time to move the pieces. Blue pieces must occupy all the open positions next to the red pieces before they can be stacked. When blue pieces were stacked three high the top piece can 'jump' over the red center pieces and continue to the opposite perimeter. Then the top pieces of two blue stacked pieces can jump until all pieces are moved.

One last "rule" was the timer also randomly provided a number from one to forty indicating which blue piece the player must begin with on the first timing event. This prevented someone from learning shortcuts or patterns that reduced the total time required for the game.

Ana noticed that you tap on the timer to restart it, much like chess players tap on a clock timer after their move. She studied the board. "Can you show me how it's done?"

Sailfish started the timer and moved pieces rapidly with one hand. It required 21 timing events to complete, and Sailfish looked exasperated. "I can usually do this in less timing events."

Ana moved all the perimeter pieces back to the other side. "Let me try."

She moved the pieces as quickly as she could and still required over 30 timer events to completely move all the perimeter pieces. "You're right it isn't easy."

She picked up the checkerboard. "Would you like to try checkers?"

Sailfish looked at his tablet. "I have a meeting I must attend. Maybe we could do that tomorrow?"

"Of course."

Sailfish left his draeger set with Ana so she could try it again if she wanted to. After the dinner meal she was bored and spent the rest of the evening trying to complete the draeger game in less than 30 timing events.

The next day, Sailfish returned and laughed when he saw Ana still trying to beat her best draeger timing events. "How are you doing with draeger?"

She smiled "I still can't beat your timer number, but I'm pretty close." She had set up the checkboard on her bed and swapped the draeger set with the checkerboard on the table.

Sailfish pulled a chair to the table and Ana sat on the bed with the table between them and started explaining the few rules of checkers. They soon were playing, and Sailfish did surprisingly well. He almost beat Ana and she asked him if they could meet on some regular basis to play checkers.

Sailfish agreed and commented he knew of some Tribanis that might be interested in learning to play checkers. He added that chess looked pretty complicated and may have to wait a while.

He left and Ana's wondered why they didn't have an electronic version of draeger on their tablets. She would ask one of the computer technicians, surely, he or she would know the answer.

Chapter 25

THE SHIP

The next morning, John stopped by Ana's compartment and escorted her to the dining hall. While they were eating, she asked why no humans near the site had ever seen a sentry.

"I checked into this. Shortly after we arrived and established the perimeter fence, we received guidance from the Advisory Council to establish a sentry system and keep track of contacts with animals or possibly humans. After 30 days each site was directed to re-deploy the sentries if no contacts were recorded. No contacts with humans or animals were recorded here and the sentries were re-assigned to other security details."

"Why didn't you say this when you heard the resistance group on the southern part of the perimeter say they never saw a sentry."

"Lieutenant Adam Jones is in charge of perimeter security. He would have received the command from the Advisory Council directly. It just never was an issue for me."

She was curious, so she asked John "Do you play draeger?"

He seemed surprised and shook his head. "It's too frustrating for me."

She laughed and thought. *I guess checkers and chess are not an option.*

Ana wondered aloud. "Your historian said some ships are larger than this and some are smaller. Is there any other difference?"

John thought for a moment. "There is one larger ship in North America near the former city of San Diego that was also set up to manufacture things we may need to replace over time like fusion reactors, or scout ships, or even the small equipment used for planting Madjuul plants."

"What about the small people carts, can they make those too?"

"Yes, why do you ask?"

"My former boyfriend was good at changing and fixing things. Do you think they could give him a few carts to see if he can use their power source for the cars that used to run on liquid hydrocarbon fuels? It would make a huge difference if people didn't have to rely on horses for transportation."

John thought about that. "Yes, I can ask if they can transport a few to the Houston encampment for that effort." He made a note in his tablet to follow-up with that idea.

When they finished eating, she asked "Could you show me around the ship? I've spent endless hours walking around but all I ever see is hallways and doors. By now, you know I'm not a security threat."

John stared at her for a moment. "What do you want to see?"

"I'm not an engineer, but I'd like to see the engine room, or the bridge. How about the communications room or the computer room, or even the storage area where all the outside buildings were stored? Something more than hallways and doors."

"Let me think about it."

"What is there to think about? As the head of security, I'm sure you could escort me anywhere. I won't touch anything you tell me not to touch."

He nodded. "Come with me."

John carried a small silver cylinder that unlocked any door. He led her first to the ship's enormous engine room. Ana stared in amazement at the ship's engine. She later described it as an enormous maze of vessels connected with large pipes, surrounding a huge central vessel. There were display screens everywhere filled with graphic images and the now familiar Tribani text that looked like Japanese Kanji characters.

When she looked at him with a huge question mark on her face, he shook his head. "Don't ask me to explain anything. My only job here is to make sure only those with the right permission have access to this room. I do know that only a small part of this equipment is running to provide power to the ship and the surrounding buildings."

Since there were no staff to provide additional information, she asked John if she could see the ship's command bridge. He led her through a maze of hallways and doors to an elevator. When John said "bridge" in Tribani, his image appeared on a display in the elevator, and it started rising to the top level. On the way up, Ana asked "why don't you use voice recognition for doors as well?"

"It would be too hard to keep track of who can enter a specific door, and the accesses would have to be updated on too frequent a basis. Very few staff can access the bridge."

The door opened to a large circular room, and she could see the sun and a blue sky through a transparent ceiling. There were several rings of consoles with graphic displays. Again, no staff were present as there were no plans to move the ship in the foreseeable future. Ana walked around the consoles that were mostly off or blank. She looked at John, who shrugged. "I know, you only need to make sure staff here have the right access permissions."

He smiled. "Thank you."

Without any additional explanation, she asked if they could continue the tour to the communications room. John led her to the guarded communications room. Luckily, the current guard wasn't Private Wilson or anyone who recognized her, so she could pretend she hadn't been there before. This room also had several rows of consoles and was staffed with a handful of communications specialists.

She had to know "Why is this room guarded?"

"I don't know, exactly. We received orders from the Advisory Council just after we landed to provide continuous security to this area. Only the guards can let someone in and only those with approved access." He shrugged. "I think the security access cards should be enough."

This time John could describe the various functions of the specialists as many of them were security related. Ana knew just enough Tribani to recognize some of the specialists' conversations with guards on patrol, other encampments and one specialist was sending a transmission back to Tribanus. A few staff acknowledged John as they walked around but just stared at Ana. They probably had never seen a human female before.

John then led her through a door to the adjacent computer room. It was a maze of computer equipment and displays. Ana was surprised that there was only one technician present. "Where are all the computer staff?"

"Most of them work remotely. The only staff in here are usually performing maintenance tasks." He paused. "Do you still want to see the storage room – for some reason?"

"Not anymore." She looked at the technician. "Just a minute."

She asked the technician if there were any games on the tablets, like draeger. He shook his head and made a comment like requests for using computer resources for something like that would never be approved.

She smiled and returned to John. "Is there any other place you would like to show me?"

He seemed embarrassed, but asked "my room?"

Ana laughed loudly. "Lead on." She hoped his bed was bigger than Lieutenant Long's. She also wondered what the rooms approved for sex looked like…

The next day, she found a program on her tablet that listed all other personnel with tablets in the Houston encampment, their 'phone' number and even their current location. She found Barry Sailfish in the community dining room and asked to speak to him confidentially. They left the dining room and found a small room with comfortable chairs and sat down.

"Do your medical experts think it's possible for humans and Tribanis to have children?"

He laughed. "I assume there is a reason you are asking. It's not my area of expertise, of course, but I know a female health specialist expert in London who would know. Would you like me to ask her?"

"Yes, please."

Sailfish smiled.

"No, I'm not pregnant."

"It's not in my current assignment, but I would be happy to provide medical assistance if that were to happen."

Ana stood up and held out her hand. "Thank you, for keeping this conversation confidential."

Sailfish stood up and shook her hand. "Of course."

Chapter 26

NEW YORK ENCAMPMENT

Future peace negotiations with resistance movements would require travel to other Tribani encampments. Ana studied some information supplied by Morrison and counted 25 encampments in North America, 15 in South America, 17 in Europe, 4 in Africa, 4 in Australia, 5 on islands like Hawaii with the remaining 30 in Asia. Morrison took her to New York to see a large city encampment. Many Tribanis chose to live in or near a large city – as they had on their home planet. A few groups preferred remote locations near mountains or lakes. Others wanted to live in a warm place and chose islands like Hawaii.

The ship had landed in Central Park. Several skyscrapers in New York City immediately inside the electronic fence around the encampment were powered again and most utilities were working. Ana had never seen anything like that. Many of the skyscrapers still had problems (no maintenance for 15 years is a big problem), but some were still in decent shape. She saw a large number of Tribanis roaming around. Food had become an issue for the large encampment in New York as human food seemed too crude to eat and they needed time to grow their own food in Central Park.

At a nearby power distribution sub-station, Morrison showed her several small fusion reactors supplying power to the power grid. "This is what we can offer to the resistance groups. We have also been studying the water treatment plants near here and hope to have a few of those functional soon."

He anticipated her next question. "Yes, we are looking at the power and water treatment plants near Houston. We should have some in operation soon."

Ana felt some sense of accomplishment in her peace agreement efforts. All humans would benefit if power and water could be restored.

After the power plant, Morrison and Ana returned to Manhattan and entered a former luxury hotel overlooking Central Park. The former hotel restaurant had been converted to a typical Tribani dining hall and they had a quick Madjuul dinner. Everything in the hotel was not functional yet, but the Tribani engineers had restored the elevator service and they took a quick trip to a room on the top floor to see the city at night.

As she stared out at the lights of the city below, Ana wondered what life was like in New York before the meteor storm. She was standing next to Morrison and when she looked at him, he took her in his arms and kissed her. She kissed him back and he picked her up and carried her into the bedroom.

The next morning, Ana woke up and Morrison was gone. There was a handwritten note on his pillow that he had to address some urgent security concerns in the London encampment, and that he would return in a day or so. She noticed that the bed sheets seemed freshly laundered, not at all like the dusty and dingy sheets she had seen in the houses near Sam which hadn't been touched in 15 years. She wondered if Morrison had planned this as a part of their visit and laughed. She dressed quickly and went to the nearest security station looking for more information about London.

Most of the Tribanis in the security station had seen her with Morrison and didn't pay much attention to her. A few stared. There were no other humans in the New York encampment. She asked around and someone told her there were rumors the London encampment had suffered a major attack the previous night but there were no details yet. She hurried to the Tribani security headquarters building in the encampment but couldn't find anyone who even knew Morrison. In the early afternoon, she sat down in a chair in a security meeting room trying to figure out what to do next and was surprised when she saw Lieutenant Long coming toward her with a very long face. She had been around Tribanis long enough to know when something was wrong.

"I'm afraid I have some bad news."

Ana felt a sense of dread as Long continued. "The London encampment was attacked again this morning and Captain Morrison was killed along with most of his security team."

Ana just stared at Long, unable to speak or move.

"There is a lot of confusion and some anger at humans, so I was ordered to come here and bring you back to the Houston encampment, for your protection."

Ana was in a daze but followed Long to a small transport. "How did you know where to find me?"

"Your communicator has a tracking device inside it." Each site peace treaty negotiator was given a communication device to allow them to ask questions or seek follow-up information from the Tribani peace negotiation team, which Ana lead.

Back in Houston, Long suggested she rest for some time while the Tribani leadership figured out a path forward. A few days passed without any update and Ana wondered if they would abandon the peace negotiations and retaliate for the attack in London.

There was a news and information channel available on almost every monitor in the ship and Ana watched it from time to time as she was becoming somewhat fluent in the Tribani language. Reports described how a resistance group near London managed to resurrect an old defensive missile launcher and sent several missiles into the London encampment. This was by far that most serious attack yet on an encampment. Dozens of Tribanis were killed including the queen and the prince's future wife, but the king and the prince had survived. There were unofficial statements about possible retaliatory attacks on all resistance movements and Ana wondered if all negotiations would end.

She retreated to her sleeping quarters to try and figure out what to do next. Should she try to escape and go back to her original group or wait it out and see what happened? The Tribanis retaliation had been rather extensive in the area around the London encampment. Initial assessments indicated the resistance had paid dearly for their attack. Nevertheless, the normally low-key Tribanis in the London encampment were concerned about their own future. They certainly did not want an all-out war and let their leadership know it, which probably prevented an even greater retaliation.

While she was waiting for the Tribani leadership to decide a future course of action, Ana accessed the Tribanis historical database in the officer's conference room. Maybe it would help her understand them if she understood their history and culture better. She was now proficient enough to listen to or read their historical records and happened to find the third survey visit to England in 1895.

The survey team consisted of a military leader, an engineer, and a historian. Each team member had specific information to collect. The military leader and the engineer dictated their notes and spoke in a thick accent that Ana could not understand. Fortunately, the historian George Watkins reportedly lost his dictation device and was forced to write notes that Ana could read.

Watkins and the other team members were very much aware of what had happened to the first survey team that, despite their best efforts to avoid contamination, had contracted diseases and most had died miserably on the return to Tribanus, leaving only their dictated records and numerous vegetables, human blood and biological samples taken during the survey. This team avoided contact with humans whenever possible and was probably saved by almost 900 years of DNA modifications that made them somewhat resistant to the bacteria and microorganisms of Earth.

Historian George Watkins major accomplishment was breaking into a bookstore one night to find several historical books including an extensive history of England. As he thumbed through it, he realized it was a lot more detailed than anything the previous surveys had brought back. He also found several books that taught children to read and write English. Watkins also mentioned that Captain William Holloway was focused on assessing the military's capabilities and the utilization of police to maintain order. The third member of the team, Samuel Jones was an engineer, and his focus was on design of buildings, the road system, bridges - basically any engineered construction.

Watkins finished his report by apologizing for his crude notes made from memory as he lost his dictation device. During the second night of the survey, the team took shelter from a rainstorm in a large house that had just been finished and the next morning, Watkins could not recover his recording device. He had fallen asleep against a large wooden cabinet and the recording device had apparently come out of his pocket and rolled under the cabinet. He and Jones tried to move the cabinet, but it was too heavy. Captain Holloway warned them of workers nearby and they left quickly before they could recover the recording device.

Ana reflected on Watkins' report and tried again to listen to the military and engineering reports. She finally gave up and sat wondering if she would have another opportunity to discuss possible peace negotiations with them or would be forced to leave and return to her old resistance movement.

Lieutenant Long stopped by each day to check on her, and Ana took the opportunity to ask about Morrison.

"What happens when someone dies, like Captain Morrison?"

Long seemed reluctant to discuss it but offered several options. "Family members are contacted, and their desires are usually followed. In Captain Morrison's case, he had no immediate family so the standard military protocols were followed. In the past, burials with appropriate ceremonies were possible, but now these activities outside a city on Tribanus are not possible, so the body is…" She paused to think of the English word, so Ana volunteered "Cremated?"

"Yes."

"But burials on Earth are possible."

"Yes, but rituals like that have long been abandoned, and I think that was not done."

Long's communication device chimed, and she told Ana she had to go. Ana sat thinking about Morrison and wondered if they had at least provided some sort of memorial to him. She sighed and walked slowly back to her room.

Another day passed without any direction from the Advisory Council on the future of peace negotiations and Ana again browsed through the Tribani historical database. She accidentally came upon a Romani engineering report on the design and usage of the Romanis' meteors used to deliver the memory affecting chemical. A note at the bottom of the report indicated this was intercepted by the stayer's spy.

The meteors were spheres consisting of hundreds of layers of large interlocking triangle pieces held together with a heat resistant binding agent or glue. Each large triangle was filled with the chemical and released it from holes on the side of the piece when it separated from the other pieces. As a meteor encountered the Earth's upper atmosphere, the heat and friction would peel off the outmost layer and burn the glue so the large pieces would separate. As viewed from the ground the meteor would appear to leave a bright shiny trail of particles as it passed over the earth. The large metallic triangular pieces continued to break apart into hundreds of smaller triangles that dispersed the chemical as they fell through the atmosphere. The falling pieces continued to break apart until they were as small as dust when they finally hit the ground. There was even an engineering drawing for comparison purposes, showing the initial size of the meteor to be at least 20 times the height of a Romani.

One related image showed a box-like attachment on a sphere that was described as a navigational aid. Ana took that to mean it could alter the direction of a sphere as it neared the Earth.

Anna sat thinking of that night. She was only seven at the time and vaguely remembered seeing the meteors streaking through the sky. At the time, her mother said the meteor shower wasn't all that different than other meteor showers in the past. No one knew at the time how this meteor shower would impact the lives of so many people.

After a few days, there was a report on the information channel that major discussions among the king and his advisory council had finally concluded that an all-out war with the humans would set back their plans for many years and there was a significant chance they would not survive on Earth. The report ended with some talk about possible negotiations.

There was also a brief notice that Lieutenant Long had been made temporary site security leader for the Houston encampment, following the death of Captain Morrison.

Chapter 27

ANOTHER FAREWELL

At the start of another lonely and miserable day, Barry Sailfish stopped by to check on her again. Her door was open, and she was sitting on her bunk. He was stunned to see that she had been crying – something rarely seen among Tribanis. He knocked before entering, which kind of surprised her, as most Tribanis had not adopted that cultural norm.

"How are you, Ana? The death of Captain Morrison was a shock to everyone. I know you spent a lot of time with him."

That question was also different as only a few Tribanis used only her first name. She also noticed he was wearing a red outfit this time, sort of like a security guard, but not the same. Even his shoes were red.

"Ok, I guess. Just waiting to hear about the future of peace negotiations, which are now not too likely."

"Perhaps, but I wanted to answer a question you asked and tell you something."

She looked up, wondering if it was more bad news.

"My female health specialist friend in London thinks it is possible for humans and Tribanis to conceive children, but the likelihood is less than humans only. She said she couldn't be more specific. I forwarded her reply to your tablet."

Not an issue now, she thought. When she didn't say anything, Sailfish continued.

"Also, I'm being transferred to another encampment. The lead medical advisor in the Los Angeles site has become ill and I will be replacing him."

She just shook her head. She didn't know too many Tribanis and now she was losing another.

When she didn't say anything, he continued. "It is an advancement for me, and an order which I cannot refuse."

She nodded and stood up, expecting him to leave but he continued. "There is one other thing I want to discuss."

He held out his hand and there were two tiny filters in his palm, the same as Captain Morrison had been given.

"My leader told me about your…" he struggled with the words and Ana finished his sentence.

"Pheromones."

"Yes, and their apparent effect on Tribani males."

Oh, oh. She thought. She wondered if there might be consequences if someone in a leadership role thought she was using that to her advantage.

Sailfish saw the concern on her face and laughed. "Since I will no longer be at this encampment, I would like to accept your offer to exchange examinations."

That caught her off-guard. She didn't know what to say, so he continued. "While I think there would be many useful things to learn from a medical examination, I would like to exchange purely physical examinations with you. If you agree."

She was trying hard to think of a reply and the only thing she could think of was. "Where?"

He closed her door and locked it. "How about here?"

Surely, he couldn't be serious. "Now?"

"I must leave tomorrow and still have some preparations for leaving."

She decided to see if he was wearing filters, so she walked to him, put her arms around him and kissed him. He kissed her back and she felt his hands wandering all over and she knew that he was wearing filters.

It took only a few minutes before they were sharing her tiny bunk. It wasn't very big, but they weren't lying on it next to each other.

As he was getting dressed, he looked at her. "That was the most pleasing examination I have ever been given."

She laughed. This diversion from her remorse over Morrison was wonderful but she knew there was little likelihood of another as he was leaving soon. He waited until she was dressed before opening her door. They kissed one more time and he said, "I hope the negotiations continue and you put Los Angeles high on your list of sites. I would like to see you again."

She kissed him once more and watched him walk off. He even turned and waved goodbye to her. He was certainly different than most Tribani males.

She sat back down on her bunk. That encounter was totally unexpected. She didn't like to make comparisons but making love with Sailfish was very different than Morrison. Later, if asked, she would have to say Morrison was more "procedural" where Sailfish seemed open to whatever she wanted.

Now, all she could do was wait to see what the Tribani leadership decided on the future of the peace negotiations. She also tried to remember when her last period was.

Chapter 28

PRINCE PHILLIP

Three more days passed, and Ana had slowly sunk into a deep depression after the death of Morrison and the departure of Barry Sailfish. She had been in captivity for more than 9 months and the only thing that had kept her going was her growing relationship with Morrison. Her encounter with Sailfish had helped for a while, but now she was sitting on her bunk just staring off into space when Prince Phillip entered (without knocking). She didn't even turn to look at him, so he pulled a chair over and sat down in front of her. She looked at him. Even in her sadness, Ana was still quite different than any other human woman he had seen. He saw why Morrison gushed over her in his routine reports. Dark curly hair and eyes, she was wearing makeup and some colorful and fashionable clothes. He also noticed her bright red lipstick and her hourglass figure, something he hadn't seen on human females before.

"I was as sorry to hear about the death of Captain John Morrison as you were. He was once the captain of my personal security, and he was my friend as well. My name is Phillip. I've wanted to meet you for some time, but there were many pressing problems I had to take care of first."

This Tribani was different. Instead of the usual security uniform he was wearing a well-tailored and colorful outfit. Maybe he was a member of the king's advisory council? She was still in a fog and just stared so he continued. "My father and I have had several conversations about you, and we know we can't keep you like this forever. So,

I'm here to offer you a choice. You can either join us and become an intermediary in future negotiations with the resistance movements or we'll release you somewhere far away from here where you won't be able to help the resistance fight us. It's your choice. You can think about this for a while and let me know of your decision. I'm hoping you'll join us."

This must be the prince that Morrison mentioned several times. "I was sorry to hear about the queen and your future partner. I know it must have been a difficult decision for you and the king to continue with negotiations."

Phillip nodded. "Very difficult. Despite the terrible attack on our London encampment, we are still willing to offer humans technology if they agree to end this conflict. We will restore power locally whenever an agreement is reached and work with local leaders to re-start the water treatment plants. We will also establish a new communication system and make it available to every group that reaches an agreement."

Ana was thinking about it as Phillip got up to leave. "You can think about it and let me know."

Phillip was a little taller than Morrison, slender and not as muscular. As Tribanis go, he was kind of cute. He turned toward the door to leave.

"Phillip, wait!"

He turned around, waiting for her reply as she stood up.

"I think I've already proven that I can negotiate with the resistance movements. Captain Morrison and I already had a plan to start negotiations in New York and several other sites."

"Yes, I know this."

"Negotiations for all the Tribani encampments could take years."

"That is probably true as well."

"So, what's in it for me?"

Phillip looked perplexed at that question. "I'm not sure what you mean."

"There is a third alternative. I could just go back to a small town near here and live quietly with some friends for the rest of my life."

It suddenly dawned on him how difficult the peace treaty negotiations would be without her and there was a high probability that they could fail. He had just assumed, given the alternative of living far from her home, she would take on the lead negotiator's role. All his discussions with his father and their meetings with the advisory council had assumed peace negotiations were a viable path forward. He suddenly realized she was negotiating with him.

"What do you want?"

She was tired of living in the Houston encampment and seeing New York had made her want more than some simple recognition of her achievements. Then she remembered that she had put on her makeup and some perfume that morning, just to make her feel better. It had worked, for a while.

"Two things. It will be very difficult to negotiate with some resistance movements as their leaders will not take me seriously unless I have some official role or title. So, I need that. And, at the end of all negotiations, I want something more for me than a 'thank you.'"

Phillip smiled. He was beginning to see why Morrison praised her work as a negotiator. He could also see why Morrison had talked about her so much and even asked one of the advisory council members about possible legal arrangements in the future should humans and Tribanis form some sort of relationship. Phillip didn't realize Ana was slowly moving closer to him until she was standing right in front of him.

"An official role is not a problem. As for what you want at the end…what do you have in mind?" He was starting to feel dizzy for some reason.

"I want what everyone wants. Something meaningful to do, a nice place to live, friends to share it with and most importantly a close personal relationship with the right person."

Phillip was feeling faint as Ana was now very close to him. His eyes suddenly glazed over, and he was staring off into space. Ana smiled, as she didn't even have to hug him. Since he was in a trance of sorts, she put her arms around him and kissed him on the cheek and lips. She sat back down on her bunk and waited for him to come to his senses.

Eventually, Phillip saw Ana sitting on her bunk. "What just happened?"

"You agreed to all my terms."

"I did? What terms?"

"You agreed to take me to London and meet your father and the Advisory Council before the next round of negotiations."

Phillip frowned. "And when negotiations are done?"

"If the negotiations are successful and future conflict is avoided, you said you would give me whatever I want – within reason of course."

"I said that?"

"Yes. We even kissed to seal the deal."

Phillip was extremely skeptical of that. Even in personal relationships, Tribanis rarely hugged, and would almost never kiss, unless they were alone. Kissing a stranger would never happen. Ana saw the skepticism written on his face. She had a small purse near her and pulled out a compact and showed him his reflection in the mirror. He was shocked when he saw her lipstick on his face.

"I…need to leave now."

Ana shrugged. "Okay. Let me know when we can go to London."

Phillip nodded, but he was still reeling from the encounter as he hurried out the door.

Ana looked in the compact's mirror to check her makeup and smiled. After a few miserable days, things were starting to look up.

Chapter 29

LONDON ENCAMPMENT

A few days later, Long led Ana to a large transport for the trip to London. This was much larger than the small scout ships she had frequented. On the way to the transport, Long updated Ana that 5 small people transporters had been delivered to the Houston encampment and several former resistance members had driven them back to the former resistance headquarters for Sam to try and retrofit their power sources into cars and trucks.

Ana said goodbye to Long and entered the ship, looking around for Phillip. The ship's second in command greeted her, escorted her to the bridge, and directed her to a seat. It was unusual as the bridge was usually reserved for the command staff. The bridge had several large windows and Ana enjoyed the view as the ship lifted off and headed for London. She wondered where Phillip was but the few command staff she asked did not know.

When the ship landed inside the London encampment, Ana was escorted off again by the second in command and was met by a member of the Advisory Council. He even held out his hand which surprised Ana, but she shook it. Ana had observed that some Tribanis were more willing to adopt human customs than others. He motioned her to follow him, and they chatted as they headed for the main building.

"Greetings Ana Cordoba, my name is Paul Mainer. I am the current Advisory Council leader. I was a good friend of John Morrison, as I know you were, and was very sad to hear of his death."

"Yes. He was a very good friend. What exactly happened here?"

"A local resistance group has attacked this site many times in a number of different ways. Some days ago, at night they launched a small rocket that landed near the power center, temporarily knocking it off-line. That's when we contacted Captain Morrison for help as his site has experienced several such attacks."

Ana tried not smile as Paul was probably describing a mortar attack not all that different than the attack she and Arun had made to "get their attention".

"Not long after Captain Morrison arrived there was another attack but this one was much more serious as it appears the group found and restored an old defensive type of rocket launcher to working condition. They managed to shoot four rockets at this site. One of them landed near the security building where Morrison and others had been discussing possible strategies including a counterattack. Another rocket landed near the main compound, killing several inhabitants including the queen and Prince Phillip's future partner, but missing the king and Prince Phillip."

"These buildings seem pretty strong. How did the rockets kill so many?"

"The security team had just finished a meeting and were leaving to discuss possible strategies with the advisory council when the first rocket landed. The queen and Prince Phillip's future partner were leaving the food center when a second rocket landed nearby. It was just a very unfortunate series of events."

"I heard there was a strong response."

"Yes, the prince and the council approved the counter measures. You probably heard about that."

"Yes, it was on the news and information channel very often."

"There was a lot of discussion on the best path forward before we all agreed to give negotiations one last chance."

The burden Ana felt to make the negotiations successful suddenly seemed to grow bigger when she heard Paul say the Tribani were giving negotiations "one last chance." She still hadn't seen Phillip when they arrived at the main building. "Have you seen Prince Phillip?"

"No. I was expecting him to be with you."

Paul led her to a large well-appointed conference room used solely by the Advisory Council. The whole council of 20 advisors were there to meet her. Each advisor had a specific area of specialization and the king and prince relied on them for guidance in that area. The whole council met when there were issues that covered several areas of specialization.

They were all standing in small groups chatting and she was a little overwhelmed as Paul led her around introducing her to the advisors. All seemed pleased to meet her, a few even shook her hand. She briefly wondered where Phillip was, but Paul asked if she would address them with details on the upcoming negotiations. Paul asked everyone to be seated and she began her summary in English hoping they would understand. She didn't know each advisor had a translating device in one ear that translated her speech to Tribani in real time.

She began slowly, describing the early negotiations with her own group and ended with a summary of the plan she and Morrison had developed for New York and the other encampments in New England. Assuming those were successful, they would move on the rest of the North American sites.

One advisor asked how long it would take to cover all the Tribani sites. She replied that it depended on the successes along the way, but probably several years.

At that point, Phillip entered wearing some colorful yet 'regal' looking clothing. Ana was surprised when the council members rose from their seats and bowed to him. She had never seen any Tribani bow to anyone. The Tribani security members greeted each other with something resembling a hand salute but they didn't bow even to superior officers.

Phillip had entered as Ana was answering the question on how long negotiations would take to cover all the Tribani sites.

When the council members sat down, Phillip thanked Ana for her help so far and then named her a Tribani title that translated to Duchess. As Phillip described it, she would be able to negotiate with each resistance group and when some minor changes or conditions were needed to the basic agreement, Ana was authorized to speak for the King and the council and make binding agreements as needed.

Ana didn't know that Phillip had already discussed her request for an office or title in a general way with his father and the council, but today he was making it official, so there would be no misunderstandings later. Ana was surprised how quickly her request for an office or title had now become official policy. She wondered what Phillip would agree to when she was done. She would have plenty of time to think about that.

After the meeting, Paul joined Ana and Phillip for dinner. She had high hopes for the food in London as she had grown tired of the Tribani food in Houston. Surely the food served to the royal family would be the best available. She couldn't believe it when they served Paul, Phillip and her the same bland yellow food she had become used to in Houston. Phillip noticed her expression.

"Is there something wrong?"

After being appointed to such a high position, it probably wasn't a good time to complain about the Tribani food, but Ana did. "I sure thought they would serve you and your father something a little tastier than this. This is what we eat every day in the Houston encampment."

Paul asked, "what's wrong with it?" He wasn't aware of anything better.

"It's almost tasteless, like mush."

Paul saw Phillip frown and pulled out a digital translation device and repeated her comment in Tribani to Phillip. They both laughed. Phillip challenged her. "We have tried human food and find it to be almost inedible." Paul had also tried human food a few times and nodded.

"That's because most human food went bad when power was lost. What's left today is pretty bad if you don't know how to prepare it properly."

"Do you know someone who can prepare it properly?"

"I can."

"You can?"

"Yes, because I learned to cook with spices, and I can do a lot better than this." She pointed to the Tribani dishes on the table.

Phillip and Paul were both skeptical, and Phillip replied, "We doubt this."

"I'm willing to bet I can make something better, from food near here."

Phillip looked confused. "What does that mean?"

"In a friendly bet both sides agree to something the other has to do if they lose the bet."

Paul was curious. "What would you do if you lose this bet?"

Ana thought about that. "I'll serve you both dinner for a week."

Phillip was intrigued at the idea of a bet. "And if I lose the bet?"

"You have to kiss me."

Phillip was surprised but Paul was shocked at the idea. "You must be making a joke."

"No joke. So, is it a bet?" She was looking at Phillip.

Paul was looking at Phillip and shaking his head, but Phillip agreed. "It is a bet."

"Ok, I'll need a few days to gather some spices and basic ingredients. I'll need some help with that as I'm sure we'll have to go into old London and find a food store to get what I need."

Paul looked at Phillip. "Are you serious about this bet?"

Phillip laughed. "Yes. I would like to see what flavorful human food is like." Paul just shook his head. Phillip noticed Ana was smiling as she made notes on her digital tablet. There was a lot he didn't know about Ana Cordoba. He was strangely intrigued to know more about her.

Chapter 30

MEAL PREPARATION

The next day, Ana met Lieutenant Long when she arrived on a scout ship from Houston. Ana needed someone familiar with her food and clothing shopping habits and she kind of missed Long. She was the closest thing to a friend she had after her brief relationship with Captain Morrison. Long was carrying a large backpack filled with items Ana had requested and took it off as she approached Ana. She had been around humans enough to adopt some of their habits and held out her hand. Ana hugged her instead, which greatly surprised her. They both laughed and started walking to the main building.

"So, what do you think about my bet with Prince Phillip?"

"It's an interesting idea. I also heard about your new role and title. Congratulations, Your Grace."

Ana smiled. "I asked for an official role in the negotiations, and they decided on that. I'm still not sure what that means to the average Tribani."

"It is a royal title, which everyone respects."

"Ok, but I would rather you call me Ana when we are alone."

"Yes, Your Grace…err Ana, if you will call me Sarah."

"Of course. So, has power been restored in Houston?"

"In some areas to the South and West of Houston. There are a lot of problems connecting a power source to a system that has been down for years, but our engineers learned a lot in the New York encampment and are working through it in the Houston encampment." She thought for a moment. "Do you remember the resistance group to the South of the Houston encampment and Kaito Tanaka?"

Ana thought for a moment. "Yes. Did they finally agree to the terms of the peace agreement?"

"Yes, and Kaito brought two engineers to the signing who wanted to help restore power. Kaito said they used to work for NASA. Do you know what that is?"

"Yes, it was a government agency that led the effort to explore planets and moons near Earth. Are the engineers helping restore the power?"

"Yes, together we are making a lot of progress. They know a lot about the old power grid."

"That's great. How have you been? I know you are also working on restoring the water treatment plants."

"Very busy. I have been working closely with several members of your former resistance group, and it's going well." She laughed, and Ana turned to her. "One of them has been very nice to me. He even gave me this." Long pulled up the sleeve of her uniform and showed Ana a silver bracelet. "It's nice, but I'm not sure why he gave it to me."

"He gave it to you because he likes you."

Ana wasn't sure Tribanis could blush, but it seemed that Long did blush. Ana wondered which one of her former group would have done that.

"Who gave it to you?"

"Arun Patel."

That surprised Ana as Arun had been one of the most vocal about harassing the Tribanis to get them to leave. She wondered if human male pheromones affected Tribani females. She explained pheromones to Long and then asked if she felt any change when she was around Arun. She blushed again and seemed to struggle for the right word. She then said a Tribani word that translated to "aroused".

That surprised Ana and she laughed. Although Long was a friend, Ana decided to keep the exact effect from her. No one needed to know she had sometimes used the effect to her advantage. "That's the exact opposite of what I've seen so far. Tribani males seem to go almost into a trance around me."

They both laughed at the difference.

"Are you dating Arun?"

Long stared for a moment. "Dating?"

"Going out to places together, eating together – just spending time together."

"Sometimes after our meetings about restoring the water treatment plant we have a meal together."

"Has he kissed you?"

Long blushed again. "On the back of my hand a few times."

Ana normally would not interfere, but she gave her some advice. "If you like him, the next time he kisses you on the back of your hand, kiss him on the lips."

Long seemed shocked and shook her head. "Oh, I don't know."

"Try it, you might like it."

Seeing Long's bracelet reminded Ana that Sam had never given her any jewelry, or anything personal like that. *Jerk!*

To be fair, Sam once told her all the jewelry stores had been stripped clean a long time ago. Paper money was thought to be worthless, but certain things like jewelry could be traded for food or other needed goods.

They were now nearing the main building when Ana remembered why Long was there. "About the bet, I need your help to get a scout ship and a small security team to go into old London and find a food store."

"I'll start on that immediately."

"Did you find everything on the list I sent?"

She handed the backpack to Ana. "Almost everything. I couldn't find some of the spices you want."

"That's okay. I'm sure we can find them in old London."

Long then handed Ana a note from Sam thanking her for the people transporter carts and said he was optimistic that the power packs could be used to replace internal combustion engines, and he was trying to retrofit his car first.

They parted ways and Ana met Long and four well-armed security experts the next morning. Long handed her a tablet with an aerial map of downtown London.

"There are no specific records of food stores, but we can start in the major shopping areas. I asked around and someone suggested Piccadilly Circus or Leicester Square as possible starting points."

Ana studied the map. "Let's try Piccadilly Circus first."

They entered the transport and a few minutes later landed in the former tourist attraction. It seemed strange to see such a developed area that once teemed with shoppers and tourists, now strangely silent and deserted. The four guards took up positions around them as they walked past numerous stores.

They finally found a small grocery store and two guards took up sentry positions outside while the others started to precede them to the store. The windows were still intact as was the door. Ana started to ask one of the guards to break a glass panel on the door, but Long interrupted her.

"That won't be necessary." She held up a metal device with a flat plate on one end and metal spider-like legs on the other end. Each leg of the spider had several small flashing lights on it. She pushed the legs into the lock and turned the flat plate and they heard the lock click. Ana motioned, and she handed it to her.

Ana examined it carefully "what is this?"

"It is a smart key that figures out how a lock works, when you insert it."

Ana smiled and handed the smart key back to Long "I know a lot of people who would like to have one of these."

It was dark inside and there was a strong rancid smell. Ana had prepared for this, and they all put on protective masks as they entered. She pulled a small flashlight out of a handbag, cranked it and picked up a basket from a stack of baskets near the front door. She found some spices she needed and several kinds of pasta in cans and plastic bags. She also found a few other things that might come in handy later.

She signaled to Long and they took off their masks as they closed the door on the way out. As they walked back to the scout ship, they passed a clothing store.

"I'd like to look in here for a few minutes."

Long was standing near two guards and replied "Yes, Your Grace." Long had informed them of Ana's new title when she arranged for the ship and the security detail.

The same security procedures were followed, and Ana soon found some interesting outfits wrapped in plastic in the storeroom in the rear of the store. Long found a shopping bag on a rack near the front door and Ana dropped her newly found clothing in the bag. Moments later they were in the scout ship on the way back to the encampment.

Long set the shopping basket on a table in the royal dining hall and waited for Ana. She soon entered the hall with a handbasket of leafy greens and some vegetables and set it on the table next to the shopping basket. Long pulled a carrot from the handbasket. "What is all this, Ana?"

"I described a garden to one of the perimeter guards and asked if he had seen anything like that and he showed me a large one, not too far from the fence. It was a little overgrown with weeds, but it had everything I need to make a salad."

"Salad?"

"A salad used to be the first thing served before a meal. It's a bunch of different vegetables served with a creamy topping for added flavor."

Long watched Ana pull everything out of the shopping basket. "Did you find everything else you need?"

"Not exactly. I would have preferred a few different spices and maybe some different basic materials, but these will do."

"Yesterday, I contacted the royal chef and described your bet with the prince. He and his staff are eager to see what you want to do and help you if they can. They said they had also never had any human food they liked."

Ana laughed. "I understand that completely."

Chapter 31

KITCHEN

The next morning, Long led Ana to the royal kitchen where they met the royal chef. She was surprised when he bowed slightly and shook her hand.

"It is a great pleasure to meet you, Your Grace. Please, let me show you around."

He proudly showed her around his kitchen and introduced her to his staff. Some food preparation equipment was different, others were the same. Ana briefly wondered why they needed such a well-equipped kitchen when all they made was the same tasteless, boring Madjuul dish.

Long handed Ana the shopping basket and handbasket and they spread everything she needed on a large metal table. Long received a message and left briefly as Ana started preparing spaghetti (which surprisingly still had a vacuum seal inside the can) as a second course. The kitchen staff gathered around to watch her make spaghetti and tomato-based sauce. When she poured the spaghetti into a colander to drain it, all the staff made gurgling noises and one ran to the sink to barf. When she poured the tomato sauce on the spaghetti, the chef had his hand over his mouth, shook his head then ran off. Ana wondered what was going on, until Long returned to the kitchen. She saw the plate of spaghetti and sauce, made a face and started laughing at the kitchen staff who were trying to hide behind racks and large equipment in the kitchen.

"What's wrong with everyone, Sarah?"

Long whispered to her. "Sorry, Ana, but that looks like morass."

Ana frowned. "The word morass means a bad situation that's difficult to get out of. It must mean something else to you."

"On our world we struggled for years to get rid of it, with chemicals and with eradication. Some still suffer from it". She continued to explain and finally Ana got it.

"That sounds like tapeworms."

Long just stared at her.

"People who eat undercooked foods or drink contaminated water sometimes ingest things that turn into tapeworms in their digestive system. There aren't many symptoms until they show up in excrement."

Long made a face. "You know all that and still eat this?"

"You can't get tapeworms from this and there are medicines or used to be medicines that took care of that. It really wasn't that big a problem."

Long made another face and shook her head. "I would not serve that to the prince…"

Ana smiled. "I know that now, but I have a backup dish."

She had prepared a large pot of scallop-shaped macaroni and cheese with some extra spices and showed it to her.

Long leaned over and smelled it. "That smells very good."

"Want to try it?"

"Oh, yes."

Ana pulled several forks from her vegetables basket and served Long a bowl and she pulled a chair next to a large table and gingerly tasted it. She soon was gobbling it down. Some of the kitchen staff and the chef wandered over and watched her eat. Ana asked them if they wanted to try it and everyone did, even the chef. They all stared briefly at the forks that Ana handed them but soon they were all eagerly eating the pasta dish.

The chef commented. "This is a very complex mixture."

"Actually, it's fairly simple. Just the macaroni and cheese and a few spices."

"Are you following a written plan or is this made up as you are cooking?"

Ana laughed. "I used a cookbook while I learned to cook for my boyfriend."

"Cookbook?"

"That's a book that tells you how to use spices to make simple things taste good."

"Do you still have this book?"

"Yes, but it would be easier to find one here in London than to retrieve that one."

Long had finished her meal and was standing next to her.

"That was delicious, Your Grace. When are you going to serve it to Prince Phillip?"

Ana thought about it. "Tonight, but I still need to make a dessert."

"Dessert?"

"Something you eat at the end of the meal. Often a dessert is sweet, but I couldn't find any sugar that was still good, so I have another idea."

Chapter 32

THE MEAL

Advisor Paul and Prince Phillip were waiting at a table in the royal dining room when Ana and Long entered carrying some covered dishes that they laid on the table.

"I couldn't find everything I wanted in old London, but I still managed to make a several course meal. We usually begin with a salad."

She uncovered a large salad nicely decorated with several vegetables. She served a plate to each who stared at it not sure how to eat it.

"You can eat it as is, or there is a dressing for the salad that makes it even more tasty."

She poured some creamy dressing over their salad plates and handed them each a fork. Phillip examined the fork then stared at the salad for a moment then looked at Long.

"Lieutenant, why don't you join us? Maybe you can show us how to eat some of the food Ana has prepared."

Ana laughed loudly, until Phillip asked. "Why are you laughing?"

"In the distant past, it was common for the king to have a 'taster' to try each dish first to make sure it wasn't poisoned."

Phillip laughed. "I'm sure that isn't the case here." He motioned Long to sit with them. She reluctantly sat down, and Ana served her a salad plate with dressing. Long hesitated, then picked up a fork and started eating the salad. They watched for a moment then followed her example.

Phillip was impressed. "This tastes much better than it looks."

After the salad, Ana served macaroni and cheese as the main entrée. It didn't look exactly like morass, but Paul and Phillip hesitated until they saw Long gobbling her plate of mac and cheese. After a few bites they both agreed it was delicious. Ana finished the meal with a plate of flourless chocolate chip cookies. Phillip picked up a cookie and noticed that it was still warm. He smelled it and slowly took a bite.

"This is wonderful." He looked at Ana who was smiling and he knew he had lost the bet. Long didn't know the consequences of losing the bet but Paul knew, and he laughed as Phillip got up, walked to Ana, and kissed her on the lips. She instinctively put her arms around him and kissed him back. Long was shocked but she tried to hide it from Paul and Ana. She was secretly relieved there wasn't anyone else in the room.

Ana noticed that Phillip was starting to stare at her, so she backed off a bit, so he could recover. At least she wasn't wearing perfume. It took a moment before he fully recovered and looked at her.

"So, what do you think of human food now?"

"I think there are things we can learn from you." He looked at the food on the table and was mentally comparing it to their own food – what Ana called "mush". He also wondered why he felt dizzy every time he was near Ana.

They all said goodnight and Long escorted Ana back to her assigned sleeping quarters.

"I think you made quite an impression on Prince Phillip."

Ana glanced at her. "You haven't seen anything yet."

Long wondered what she meant as they entered the sleeping quarters area of the main building.

Chapter 33

PHEROMONE RESISTANCE

Phillip met with Ana frequently as they worked to develop a standard peace agreement which for the humans basically meant ceasing all hostilities. Ana felt guilty about her pheromones and their effect on Tribani males, especially Phillip. She confided to him the nature of the issue and Morrison's solution. Phillip contacted the royal physician who provided him with something like Morrison's filters. Phillip decided to try them out without telling Ana. Ana instinctively tried to stay several feet away from Phillip so they could finish the basic agreement. She was surprised when he stood next to her and didn't seem to be affected. They were standing close when she suddenly put her arms around him and kissed him. He surprised her by holding her close and kissing her back.

"Someone told me Tribanis don't hug and kiss, even in private."

"That isn't always true but maybe it's time for a change."

"There are some other things I was told that Tribanis don't due except for procreation."

"That is generally true as well."

"I think you're missing out on a lot."

Phillip laughed. "Again, I think you are right."

They kissed several times, until Ana whispered in his ear, and he replied, "I know just the place."

King Henry

Ana and Phillip finalized the basic peace agreement they would start with in all negotiations. They passed it by the advisory council who made only minor changes. Ana still had not met the king and she asked Phillip when she could finally meet his father. King Henry had been ill for some time and had almost recovered when the advisory council passed the agreement subject to the king's approval.

Phillip escorted Ana to a sitting room next to his father's bedroom so she could meet him, and they could discuss the basic agreement.

Henry was sitting in a chair next to a wood-burning fireplace when they entered. Ana wasn't sure how she should address the king or greet him. She had asked Phillip who told her there was no protocol for humans since they technically were not his subjects.

Henry looked a great deal like Phillip, only older and grayer. When he saw her, he smiled and she curtsied, something no Tribani female did (they all bowed). He motioned her to come closer.

"I have heard a lot about you, Ana Cordoba, from many people. I wish I could have met you sooner, but I appear to be allergic to something here in London."

"I have heard a great deal about you as well, Your Majesty. I'm glad to finally meet you."

Phillip handed his father the final version of the agreement. "The advisory council agreed to this version earlier today."

Henry looked it over. "I'm sure this is fine as a lot a very smart people have thought about this." He looked at Phillip. "Did you tell her how you convinced the council to continue negotiations?"

Ana and Phillip looked at each other. "After the attack, there were many Tribanis who wished to settle the issue with force, but I managed to convince them that only you could make the diplomatic approach work. You seemed to have figured that out on your own and used your negotiating skills on me to obtain what you wanted."

Ana smiled. "The secret to all successful negotiations is to know more about your counterparts than they know about you."

Henry and Phillip laughed. "You were right Phillip. I don't think anyone else could make this work."

Henry motioned Ana closer. He had never seen a human female this close and was surprised by her stylish clothing and makeup. He had never seen bright red lips or red fingernails before, or a female with an hourglass figure. He had some confidential discussions with Phillip and knew that his son had become emotionally attached to her. After seeing her and listening to her, he could see why.

After a few more pleasantries, Phillip and Ana left Henry to enjoy the warmth of his fireplace. Phillip informed the council that his father agreed to the latest document and of his plans to immediately start negotiations with the groups around the New York encampment.

His presence wasn't necessary, but Phillip decided to observe the negotiations disguised as a guard. He hoped his presence wouldn't affect Ana's efforts to obtain an agreement. She didn't seem to mind when he told her of his plans.

Chapter 34

NEW YORK NEGOTIATIONS

Jason Evers, the Tribani site leader of the New York encampment, held a pre-meeting review with Ana prior to the start of negotiations for the New York area.

He bowed slightly "Greetings Your Grace, it's a pleasure to finally meet you."

They shook hands and she sat down at a conference table. Evers began by displaying an aerial map of the area on a monitor with possible locations of the resistance groups circled in red.

"On your instructions, we sent several scout ships out at night and captured a large number of humans all around the encampment that probably represent all the different resistance groups here. We gave them your request for a meeting to discuss a possible peace treaty and let them leave. So far 6 different groups have contacted the perimeter guards about attending."

Ana was studying the map. "Do you think that's all of them?"

"We think so. We also told them we would contact them when you arrived, and we were ready to start the negotiations."

So far, her plans for New York were off to a good start. "How about tomorrow?"

Evers nodded. "We'll send some ships out tonight with searchlights as a signal to let them know we are ready tomorrow.

The next day, six resistance leaders were escorted through various sections of the perimeter fence to a scout ship that had been outfitted with a large conference table. They were surprised that they were searched for weapons before they were allowed on board the scout ship. They were also acutely aware of the large security presence protecting Ana. They didn't know that one of the security guards was Prince Phillip in disguise and wearing a uniform. The other guards didn't even know Phillip was there as they had never seen him in person, only in pictures.

After a suitable round of introductions, Ana wanted to begin by talking about prior agreements with other groups. This was a tough, stubborn group however, and on seeing Ana, most of them doubted she was the lead negotiator for the Tribanis. One even commented to another that he thought she was there to serve drinks and snacks. They all started trying to see who could talk the loudest, perhaps even trying to take over the meeting.

Ana pulled out a small, compressed air foghorn and blew it several times to get their attention. She repeated her high-level historical summary of the Tribanis migration ending with the meteor shower and its effects on Tribanis and humans. She then walked around the table and handed each leader an electronic tablet displaying pictures of the affected Tribanis and ended by summarizing the peace treaty conditions agreed to by the advisory council and the king.

"I was going to give you some background information on previous negotiations that resulted in peace agreements, but it seems you aren't interested in that. So, let me make it clear. You are here to agree to several terms that have already been negotiated with other groups like yours. We are not here to start from scratch."

One of the loudest leaders asked, "Why are you helping them?"

"Because the alternative is too awful to imagine."

Another vocal leader asked, "What if we don't agree with your terms?"

She briefly described the rocket attack on the London encampment and the Tribani's forceful response. The room grew quiet, and the attendees started studying the key points of the agreement:

All hostilities must stop. Each side must be assured they are no longer in danger from an attack.

Permanent representatives will meet frequently to discuss current issues and make minor modifications to the cooperation plan.

Tribanis will provide machinery to help humans plant crops.

The Tribanis will begin connecting nuclear fusion reactors (slowly) to existing power grids to re-establish power. Once power is restored to an area, joint human and Tribani teams will work to establish clean running water to that area (which benefits both)

Both sides will work on establishing an internet-like communications system for North America

Horse transportation alternatives will be developed.

The rest of the document provided details on milestones, communication protocols and other items needed to fully implement the treaty.

"You only have to agree to stop all hostilities at this meeting. Then, the rest of the terms of the treaty will happen quickly."

It didn't take the resistance leaders long to understand their limited ability to affect the final agreement. Once they realized that, they quickly agreed to the terms of the agreement.

Prince Phillip had been in the conference room all along disguised as a security guard. There were several times he was tempted to intervene, but he decided to let Ana finish it on her own.

He left when each leader digitally signed a copy of the agreement on the tablet he was holding. Phillip returned dressed as the prince and the leaders knew he was a high Tribani official when all the other security guards bowed to him.

He introduced himself and gave a brief statement thanking Ana and the leaders for finalizing an agreement and committed the Tribanis to do their part of the agreement.

One of the leaders asked about restoring power as that seemed to be on the minds of most of the leaders. Phillip said power had also been restored to parts of Houston and that they had learned a lot from that and hoped to make it go even faster in the New York area outside of Manhattan.

The meeting ended, and Ana and Phillip were alone in the conference room.

"Impressive meeting." He picked up the foghorn and studied it. "Where did you get this?"

"Lieutenant Long found it in a hardware store near here, before she returned to Houston."

Phillip pressed the trigger and jumped at the sound. "Very effective."

Since they were alone, they started hugging and kissing.

Long and Arun

Lieutenant Long was surprised when she returned late in the afternoon to Houston and Arun was waiting for her, nominally to update her on the latest progress on restoring the water treatment plants. Long suspected there was more to it than that and thought about Ana's comments on how she should respond to Arun's actions. She suggested they go to dinner to talk about it and Arun agreed. They did discuss the treatment plant but now Long was looking for signs that Arun might be interested in more than clean water. She described her time with Ana, the bet Ana made with Prince Phillip and the results of the meal which won the bet for Ana. She didn't mention the outcome of the bet.

They had talked a long time and, on the way out of the dining hall, Arun mentioned he needed to get back to the group's headquarters before dark to avoid the wild animals. He took her hand and kissed the back of it. She immediately put her arms around his neck and kissed him on the lips. She smiled at his surprised expression. A few Tribanis walked by them, also surprised at Long and Arun's kiss. It took a few seconds, but he pulled her close and they kissed several times. Long had never experienced anything like that and she liked it. She was disappointed when Arun said he really wished he could stay longer but the sun was going down and he had to hurry.

Long watched him enter a modified people transporter and leave. She then went to the ship's library and looked up what was known about the human custom of dating. She looked forward to their next water treatment meeting and what might follow.

Chapter 35

THE NEXT NEGOTIATIONS

Following the successful negotiation in the New York area, Ana and her negotiations team started similar negotiations in the Chicago area with the Los Angeles area next on the list.

Between each effort, she returned to London to nominally report back to the Advisory Council, but she really spent all her free time with Phillip.

Ana presented a proposal to the advisory council that they create several negotiation teams to complete the remaining sites in North America, as this would greatly shorten the overall time to obtain peace agreements for all the encampments. The council agreed to work on that. They asked Ana if there were other humans who would be willing to lead those teams in the belief that the local human resistance leaders would be skeptical of all-Tribani negotiating teams. Ana promised to find some humans who would be willing to be interviewed for the role of negotiation team leaders.

While they were working on that, they began discussing the next series of negotiations for encampments in Europe where translators would be needed to ensure accuracy of the agreement. The Tribani's electronic translators had limited ability in languages other than English.

As the Advisory Council tackled that issue, Ana and the negotiations team visited the Los Angeles encampment to work on a peace agreement. While she was there, she made a point of asking about

Barry Sailfish, but he was, unfortunately, away helping the medical personnel in the Seattle encampment with a flu outbreak. She left word for him wishing him luck containing the outbreak. Tribanis had never experienced anything like that and they were struggling to contain it.

Phillip had a surprise for her when she returned from the Los Angeles negotiations. One of the council advisors was a "cultural" expert and had advised him on human norms. Phillip was waiting for Ana's transport, and they hugged in front of the ship's crew and the ground crew. Tribanis in London were becoming used to seeing them together, so they weren't too surprised when they hugged in public. They also were aware of her negotiation successes. Power was being restored as soon as each agreement was reached, and water treatment plants were coming back online. There wasn't a real need to restore power to London yet as the reprisal for the rocket attack had practically eliminated most humans in the vicinity.

As soon as they were inside, they hugged and kissed on the way to Phillip's quarters. Ana wasn't sure Tribanis developed the same kinds of emotional attachments and if it was even possible for Phillip to tell her he loved her. But this was a special night and Phillip did exactly that when he proposed to her.

King Henry was not surprised when Phillip told him he was going to form a permanent relationship with Ana. Although Tribanis had a legal arrangement known as a permanent relationship it did not have the same meaning as marriage did to humans.

Henry even offered his approval in public during an Advisory Council meeting. Once he had his father's approval, Phillip made an announcement over the news and information channel seen in all encampments of his upcoming legal arrangement with Ana (he even called it "marriage" even though the Tribanis didn't marry). This didn't surprise anyone in the London encampment as they had seen Phillip with Ana on many occasions. In the other 99 encampments, there was little reaction as it didn't have a direct impact on their lives, and they had a lot of other things to worry about. Most were aware of Ana's role in the peace negotiations, which were always favorably reported.

There was no precedent, but Ana and Phillip worked on combining Tribani traditions with human traditions. She invited all her old resistance group but didn't expect many would make the trip. She even took the unusual step of asking Long to be her maid of honor. No one had seen or heard of her sister in some time. Phillip asked Paul to be his best man and several advisory council members to be his groomsmen. Ana didn't know many human females, so Long asked some of her female friends to be Ana's bridesmaids.

Arun found a relative of a resistance group member who had been a judge who agreed to perform the ceremony (the human part). King Henry and one of the advisory council members would perform the Tribani part of the ceremony.

Long arrived a few days ahead of the ceremony and was met by Ana who wanted to go over the role of Maid of Honor with her. When Long saw Ana she bowed and held out her hand. She laughed when Ana hugged her instead.

"Congratulations on your upcoming marriage, Your Grace."

"Ana." She corrected. "Likewise, congratulations on your promotion to Captain."

"Thank you, Ana. I know that you must have helped with that decision. There are some other Lieutenants that were surprised as well."

Ana smiled. "All things are subject to negotiations."

Captain Long laughed, then asked "What is a Maid of Honor?"

"A Maid of Honor helps the bride-to-be with all the little details that make a wedding special."

"Thank you for this honor, Ana."

"I would be happy to be your Maid of Honor, someday."

Long blushed. "Yes, someday."

The wedding day finally arrived, and King Henry led a huge procession from the main ship to a wedding venue set up in an open space inside the encampment. The whole ceremony was being broadcast to all encampments and took a little less than half an hour. In human tradition, the judge asked Ana and Phillip to repeat some vows they had written, to exchange some wedding rings and then pronounced them married. He ended his part by asking them to kiss. Although kissing was still not a widely accepted practice among the Tribanis, they were becoming familiar with it and did not react at all when they kissed. King Henry and Paul took turns reading some ancient text about lifelong commitments and Henry held his hands over Ana and Phillip and repeated another ancient verse recognizing their union and wishing them a long life together. Ana and Paul then led the assembled group back to the main ship where a reception had been set up in the dining hall.

Most of the Tribanis were surprised when music began to play and some of the humans began to dance to the music. Ana even managed to get Phillip out on the dance floor for a brief period. Other traditions were modified, but Ana had worked with the royal chef to make a wedding cake of sorts (without flour) but everyone enjoyed watching them cut the cake and feed each other the first piece.

King Henry left to rest, and the reception gradually wound down until only a few older humans were left reminiscing about their weddings in the past.

Chapter 36

HAWAIIAN HONEYMOON

Ana and Phillip chose to spend a week in the Hawaiian encampment on Maui. They spent a lot of time sightseeing and generally enjoying their time together. Near the end of the week, Phillip received an urgent message from London on his personal communicator. There had been contact with a group of Tribanis who were headed to Earth and were demanding they give them supplies or they would attack encampments on Earth. Phillip and Ana were shocked but hurried back to the security center to contact London. By that time, there was an incoming message from the leader of the incoming Tribanis. Ana was standing next to Phillip when a video communication came in from the leader of the rogue Tribani ship. She was shocked at the appearance of an unchanged Tribani. His skin was red, his pupils were yellow, and his irises were red. He had long ears, and a small nose and mouth and short black hair. He was also wearing a red ominous uniform. Phillip noticed as she instinctively took a step back. He put his hand on her arm and confronted the leader in their native language.

"What do you want? Why are you here?"

The leader stared at Phillip and noticed Ana standing next to him.

"We are here to take what we need, and you will give it to us, or we will destroy any landing site that resists. We just sent you a list of what we want."

"You know you can't live on Earth."

"We have found a new planet that will serve our needs and have built an enclosed city there. After we get what we need here we will go there immediately. Tell your people to give us what we want, and we won't harm them."

"We will not give you anything."

There was a noticeable disdain in his voice. "Your people are settlers, not warriors. They have no idea of what we can and will do to them. You have only 20 sones to comply or we will begin to take what we need by force."

The screen went blank, and Phillip glanced at Ana. She was staring at him with a shocked, wide-eyed expression. "What's going on, Phillip?"

Phillip stared at the rogue group's list on his tablet. The first item was a huge amount of food. Ana noticed his expression was grim as he looked at her. "There was always a very small group of the non-leavers who were angry or envious of those leaving. After a few generations, it was too late to begin the transformation for those that changed their mind and wanted to come to Earth. We believe our old enemy, the Romanis, were working secretly with them to find a new planet in exchange for supplying the Romanis with food and water for their explorations and conquests. They must not have transported enough food to support themselves until they could grow more. When that happened, they figured they could just come to Earth and take food and water and other things they felt they needed for this new planet."

"Why didn't they bring enough of their own food, like you did?"

"This is an unofficial, even illegal, organization not sponsored or agreed to by the various governments on Tribanus. They could not just take and hide away large quantities of food for this migration. Many years ago, when our sun began to expand, and everyone was forced to live in enclosed cities, food became tightly controlled. Our migration had long been planned and accepted by the governments."

"Can we fight them? How many are there?"

"Their weaponry is probably no better than ours and based on our best estimate there are twenty ships currently in orbit. How many of them are in each ship is not known."

"What will you do now?"

"There are few choices. Our ships have been partially dismantled to make the buildings you see around the encampment. It would take several months to prepare a ship to leave Earth and engage them. We only have 20 sones or one Tribani day to reply – that's about 30 Earth hours."

"What will they do?"

"They will probably attack a single site with all their ships at once, then land and take what they want. Then they will repeat this at each landing site until they have what they want. The worst thing is not knowing which sites they will attack first."

"Could we fight them with the scout or transport ships?"

"The scouts and transports are lightly armed and no match for their ships."

"Is there any chance of avoiding a war? Could we give them what they want, so they will leave?"

"It's probably not possible to give them what they want. It's fortunate they don't know that humans survived the meteor shower. If they did, one of the things they could want is humans for laborers at their new planet."

Ana just stared at him. "Humans would not survive long on an unknown planet. Neither will they if they haven't prepared for the micro-organisms there."

"They know that, but they may be hoping the new city's enclosure will protect them from the local organisms."

Chapter 37

FOOD BONUS

Ana and Phillip returned to London. On the way, they continued to discuss possible strategies for dealing with the rogue Tribanis. Ana contacted Paul to get some key advisors together to discuss a response. Once they arrived, Phillip left to consult with his father on the issue while Ana found Paul in the Advisory Council conference room.

He bowed and then held out his hand. "Greetings, Your Highness."

She smiled and shook his hand. "Thanks. It'll take some time to get used to that. Have you heard anything else from the rogue group?"

"Yes, just a few moments ago, they sent another list of demands. Most of the new list isn't an issue, like clothing but there is a big problem with their original demand for food." He showed her the old and new lists of demands on his tablet. It was in the Tribani language, but Ana was now fluent in the language and their writing. Even as she reviewed the list, several other council members entered the conference room. They were also carrying tablets, so she knew they had the same information.

"I'm not sure of the measurement, but it seems like a lot of food."

"It is almost one-fifth of the total supply we brought with us. It took many Tribani years for us to accumulate that much food as supplies on Tribanus are very tight. This rogue group would not be allowed to accumulate food for any reason, especially when supplies were tight."

Ana knew that the Tribanis who remained were living in enclosed cities due to the extreme heat of their expanding sun. Space available for growing food was also severely limited.

"What is the impact if you gave them that much food?"

"We estimate it will take several Earth years to replace it, assuming we don't run out of food while we are trying to replace it." He noticed one council member standing next to Ana. "Your Highness, this is Mary Johnson. She is our agricultural expert. Maybe she can give you more details."

Mary Johnson was tall and slender like Captain Long and was wearing colorful clothing like Paul. She bowed to Ana and shook her hand.

"We have enough food in storage for about three Earth years. We determined that it would take that long to grow our own food from seeds and small plants, assuming it would grow in a similar time frame. If we were to give up one-fifth of it, we can't be sure we will have enough reserves to make it through the second winter."

She started shaking her head and Ana asked what was wrong.

"This rogue group probably does not know that the Madjuul seeds and plants we brought with us have been modified over many years to be compatible with soil on Earth. I don't know what will happen to them when they eat it."

"Isn't the product cooked before it's eaten?"

"Yes, but I'm not sure that's enough to make it safe for them."

Paul chimed in. "That's not our problem, is it?"

Mary laughed. "I guess not."

Five other council members were now gathered around them staring at the list of demands on their tablets, making comments like "we can't agree to this" and "this is totally unacceptable".

Ana asked them all to be seated, then continued. "What about human food? Have you totally dismissed that as an alternative to the food that we would have to give them?"

Mary spoke for the rest. "We have tried human food several times and find it not edible."

"You haven't tried human food that's been properly prepared."

Paul tried not to laugh as he had been down this path before. He knew where she was going with this.

Mary replied. "Are there any humans who know how to properly prepare human food to make it edible?"

"I do."

There was a stunned silence, so Ana continued. "Most human food went bad when power was lost. But there were humans that were always worried about natural disasters, like windstorms and floods and even the possibility of war and they stored large amounts of specially prepared food in secret locations where they could live until these problems passed. I have asked Captain Long of the Houston encampment to bring some of this food here and the royal chef has been following my instructions on how to prepare this food. I want to share it with you now."

Long had been standing by a door and as soon as the council members were seated, signaled the chef and his staff and they brought in covered trays and placed one in front of each of the council members.

"This is typical of what is available and would represent a typical human meal before the power was lost. I hope you enjoy it."

Each council member hesitated then uncovered a plate of food with several courses of food. Ana motioned to Long to sit with them and eat so they would know the food was okay. They watched Long for a moment, then picked up forks and slowly started to eat.

Paul spoke first. "This is even better than the meal you served Prince Phillip and me."

Ana smiled. "This food was prepared by experts in food preparation and storage, almost 20 Earth years ago."

All the council members were amazed and started eagerly eating the various courses until Paul summarized the results.

"I am sure we can all agree that properly prepared human food would be an excellent replacement for the food we have to give this rogue group."

Mary commented. "I agree. I just don't like the fact that an unlawful group can come here and force us to give up food and the other items on their list."

Paul saw Ana smile. "You must have something else in mind than just giving them what they want."

"I want to give them a little added bonus."

At that point, Prince Phillip joined the meeting and the council members rose and bowed to him. He heard Ana's comment about a bonus. "The King is unfortunately ill again but has agreed to let us decide how to reply to the rogue group." He looked at Ana. "What do you mean by a 'bonus'?"

Ana motioned to Long, and she placed a Tribani food storage box on the table. She bowed to Prince Phillip and opened the box. Ana laughed when most of the council members suddenly held their noses.

"So, this is what happened to most human food when power was lost. As you can see, and smell, it is no longer edible even with spices and other things that improve the flavor of food. I propose placing several boxes of this in with the Tribani food boxes sent to the rogue group, as something a little extra, and unexpected. Then, let's see how they survive this germ bonanza."

Phillip, Paul and several council members laughed.

Phillip complimented her. "That's an excellent plan. How do you want us to do this?"

"As soon as possible we need to send several boxes of ruined food to ten large encampments with instructions on how to hide it in the food pallets they will send. Then tell the rogue group we have agreed to their demands – to avoid a possible war."

Phillip saw Long standing nearby. "Can you arrange for the packages to be sent to the other encampments as quickly as possible?"

She replied. "Of course, Your Highness."

"Let me know when this has been accomplished and I will contact the rogue group. In the meantime, I need to tell my father what we are planning." He looked at Ana. "Will you come with me?"

"Of course."

The council members and Long bowed as they left and Long hurried to find the sentry who had directed Ana to the garden for her earlier meal for Phillip and Paul. It shouldn't be too hard to find spoiled vegetables.

It seemed a lot longer to Ana than 30 hours, but she was with Phillip when he called the rogue group's leader to inform him of their decision. She was careful to stand where the rogue leader would not see her.

When he came into view, he saw Phillip standing with his arms folded. "Well, what have you decided?"

"We will give you what you want, only to avoid a war which we don't want. But we have to send you the items in transports from several encampments and you can make the transfer directly to your ships. No encampment has that much food."

The rogue leader frowned. That was unexpected, but he was getting what they needed, so he didn't care. "If that is how you want to do it." He didn't see Ana this time and forgot that he wanted to ask

Phillip who she was. He wasn't sure how far the DNA conversion to human could have changed them, but Phillip didn't seem all that different from the day they all left Tribanus. He forgot to ask about Ana when Phillip changed the way they would receive what they needed.

Ten large transports lifted off and rendezvoused with the rogue vessels. The transfers were made, and the rogue ships immediately headed for their new home, totally unaware of the ticking time bombs in their cargo areas.

Chapter 38

PREPPER FOOD

Free of the impending danger and mindful they had just given up a significant portion of their stored food at the London site and nine other encampments, Ana and Long made an emergency trip to Houston to find the source of the food. The outside of the boxes brought to London had been damaged over time by a small water leak in the shelter. Fortunately, the food inside the boxes had been well sealed and preserved.

They utilized a people transporter to travel to the former resistance headquarters and Ana smiled when Long kissed and hugged Arun when they arrived. She wondered if Long had finally given in to the idea of a permanent relationship, or a possible marriage.

Power had been restored to the area west of the Houston encampment and fresh water was now starting to flow. It seemed strange to see the few former resistance members that were left, moving about in the daylight without fear of being discovered. Most of the resistance members had returned to their homes to take advantage of the power and water to try and resume the lives they had before the meteor shower. They also had to go around from house to house and shut off power and water at the unoccupied houses to avoid electrical fires and water leaks that could flood a house with broken lines or open faucets.

They also discussed Sam's progress in utilizing the power sources in the small people transporters in a few small cars and a light pickup truck. Arun utilized one of Sam's early small car conversion successes to drive them to the underground shelter, and they were surprised to find the lights working as they entered. Ana and Long donned masks as the small water leak over time had allowed a lot of mold to grow and the smell was horrendous. Ana and Long systematically examined all the remaining boxes in the shelter looking for shipping labels until they had examined them all. They had taken pictures of the addresses of the companies on a tablet, and she showed it to Arun who was waiting outside.

"It looks like the food was purchased from six different companies and all were located either in Salt Lake City or Orem Utah. I guess we should visit the Salt Lake City encampment. They may be able to help us find some of these companies."

On the way back to the former resistance headquarters, Ana asked Arun if Sam's success could be duplicated by other former resistance teams, and he said based on Sam's progress so far, it should be possible in the near future.

She didn't see Sam pickup truck. "By the way, what happened to the truck that Sam got running?"

"We ran out of diesel. It turned out the Baytown group found a small diesel storage tank at the truck loading rack at the refinery, not one of the large tanks in the tank farm area. When they found out what we were doing they messed up the rest of the diesel trying to make a simple but unneeded distillation."

"Maybe we can restart the refinery someday." She thought for a moment. "Have you seen Sam lately?"

"He and Sheena returned to his house when the power came back on. I haven't seen or heard from him in a few days. I think he is working pretty hard on utilizing the transporter power sources in some new things. He even mentioned trying one in a motorcycle. I don't know where he found that."

They arrived back at the people transporter and Ana waited while Arun and Long hugged and kissed and said goodbye.

Long was smiling, and Ana had to know once Arun was out of sight. "Well, did you finally do it?"

Long blushed again. "Yes."

"And?"

"It was wonderful."

"Have you talked about the future?"

"He wants to marry me, I think. I'm not sure."

"What did he say?"

"I don't know. It sounded like a poem. He got down on one knee and asked me something I didn't understand and then he gave me this." She pulled out a small diamond engagement ring from her pocket. "I told him I needed time to understand all this, and he said 'okay.'"

Ana laughed. "If you agree, you're supposed to wear that on the second finger of your left hand to show everyone you intend to marry him. So, what are you going to do?"

Ana watched Long try the ring on then put it back in her pocket. "Marry him, I think."

Ana held out her arms and they hugged. "Congratulations."

Long blushed again. "Thank you, Your Highness."

"Ana…"

Long smiled and they entered the people transporter for the short trip to the Houston encampment.

Chapter 39

SOURCES OF FOOD

The next day, the Salt Lake City encampment looked to Ana just like a typical smaller Tribani encampment. Long and Ana were greeted by the site manager, now mayor, and his management team. It had taken some time, but they had slowly adopted human names for city council members. All sites had carried some video of the prince's marriage to Ana, and they bowed when they saw her. The mayor was shocked at Ana's appearance in person. They had seen very few humans and even fewer females, and when he did, they did not look like Ana.

"Welcome, Your Highness, my name is Joseph Stern."

Ana held out her hand and Stern hesitated then shook it.

"Thank you, Mayor Stern. Can we go to your council room? We need your help to find some locations here in Utah that used to make a special type of food."

"Of course, please come this way." He led them to the council room where Ana filled them in on the plan to replace the food taken by the rogue group with human food. They were immediately skeptical of that, and Ana assured them they were looking for a special type of human food, one they had probably not yet tried but would like.

They all reviewed several Tribani aerial surveys of the area, but nothing stood out as likely sites to explore. The city of Salt Lake covered over a hundred square miles and the mayor said what they were all thinking.

"Without more information, this search could take a very long time."

Long commented. "We have the actual addresses, but that doesn't help us find them on an aerial view. We need a local map."

Ana thought for a moment. "Can you identify a library building?"

The council members looked at each other without any sign they could.

"We may have to do this the hard way." She described the accepted protocol for peace negotiations with local groups and they seemed confused as there had been no attacks on their encampment and several scout ships had only found a few sites nearby that might be inhabited. It appeared that the encampment had been set up in a relatively unoccupied area just south of Salt Lake City, and it had not even been noticed by local humans who were just trying to survive. As a result, there were no local contacts who could help locate the food preparation companies.

"Could you take us to one of these occupied sites?"

"Yes, of course, Your Highness."

After a brief rest, a small scout ship took Ana and Long to a small town just outside Salt Lake City that appeared to be occupied. A small security team followed them out of the ship but once outside, Ana asked Long for her hand weapon. She wasn't sure how the weapon worked and hoped she wouldn't need it.

Long was surprised that she even asked. "I can't let you go alone, Your Highness. They would not let me live if anything happened to you."

"These people probably have never seen a Tribani and may not even know that you are here. I probably wouldn't be able to get any information out of them if they see you."

"That's why I brought this." She put on a sweatshirt and matching sweatpants she pulled from a backpack, pulled the hood over her head, and put some sunglasses on. Ana laughed.

"I didn't know you could disguise yourself. Where'd you get the clothing?"

She chuckled quietly. "From Arun. He likes this look."

Ana laughed. "Okay. Let's go."

Long ordered the security team to stay with the ship and started walking with Ana to the nearby town.

They had landed near a highway and the first building they came to was once a grocery store. There was no one around so Ana and Long entered and Ana started searching for a map or anything that might help them find the addresses of the emergency food companies. The store had been ransacked and there were some empty racks that might have held local magazines or maps at one time, but all were empty. After a quick search they moved on.

They bypassed a junkyard and a roadside restaurant that Ana doubted would have a map. They finally came to another grocery store.

"This might work."

They started to enter the store but there were several wild dogs sleeping in the entry and a few wild hogs were wandering around the parking lot in front. Ana motioned Long to move on. She didn't want to disturb the dogs or the hogs.

"I'd rather not deal with them."

Long nodded and they moved on.

They came to a former rental car lot. The office building had been ransacked but when they started searching through the office desks and file cabinets, Ana found a pad of local maps in a file cabinet. The top copies were too faded to be useful but after removing several sheets she found one that was still readable.

"Jackpot!"

Long frowned. "Is there something wrong?"

She showed Long the map "No, this is a not a very detailed city map. But it has the major roads identified, and I think one of the food preparation businesses is on the intersection of these two roads."

Long contacted the scout ship to pick them up.

After studying the map, they could easily identify most of the food preparation companies. They landed near the closest company that had a small office building in the front and a large warehouse in back. Ana asked two members of the security detail to go to the back of the warehouse in case they couldn't get in the front. The front office door was chained and padlocked. Ana was about to call the security detail to return from the back door when Long pulled out a small silver cylinder and aimed what appeared to be a blue beam at the chain. It melted and fell off the door handle.

Ana motioned Long to hand it to her and studied it. "Is this a LASER?"

Long shrugged. "I don't know what that is, but this is a type of energy beam that can cut most small metal pieces."

Ana took out her flashlight and hand-cranked it to guide them through the dark office building and followed signs to the warehouse in back. The front section of the warehouse was an extremely large and clean kitchen where food had been prepared and cooked and Ana was surprised there was no smell of rotting food. The most prominent feature in the kitchen was a huge vacuum sealing machine. There was a conveyor belt to carry the prepared bags of food to the back of the warehouse for packaging. When they entered the back part of the warehouse, Ana and Long had to stop and stare in amazement at the floor-to-ceiling racks that were almost full of boxes. A warehouse robot had apparently been used to load and unload the shelves with boxes of food.

Long commented "this is probably more food than three large encampments brought."

Ana examined the nearest boxes and confirmed they still had several more years until the expiration date.

"Okay. We need to start loading this on the ship. Can you have them land by the back door?"

"Yes, Ana." In moments the scout ship landed near the warehouse's back door that Ana and Long had opened. The security team found and loaded several small carts and pushed them to the ship as soon as the outside door opened.

"Do you want to take all of this now?"

"We'll take some of it now. We'll need the large transport to get it all."

When they returned to the Salt Lake City encampment, the mayor and city council members gathered around one of the carts and watched as Ana opened a box. She chuckled quietly as the whole box was full of plastic packages of cooked spaghetti. When she held up a package, Long laughed when the mayor and council all backed up and most put their hands on their mouth.

"This is not morass, trust me." Ana opened another box and found bags of dried fruit and vegetables. She looked at Long "You might like this."

"Another salad, Your Highness?"

"Yes, but much better than I could prepare."

The rest of the council had slowly drifted away. Some almost ran to get away, leaving Ana and Long to open a few more boxes. "This is excellent. Sarah, could you ask the head chef here to help us prepare a dinner for the council tonight?"

Long looked around and realized that everyone else had left them alone. Unlike the vegetables in Ana's salad, the vegetables in the bags looked bright and fresh and more colorful.

"Immediately, Ana. I'm sure they will be surprised at the quality of the food."

That evening, the mayor and council members reluctantly agreed to try the prepared human food. They had not liked the little human food they had tried, but they didn't want to say no to a Princess. The chef and his staff delivered a multi-course meal to the mayor and council members and Long placed a fork next to each plate. The mayor picked it up and studied it. They saw Long sit down and start eating her salad and one by one each gingerly tried the salad, then the main course and ended with a dessert.

The mayor commented. "This is unexpectedly good."

"Tomorrow, I'd like to come up with a plan to find the other food preparation companies here in Salt Lake and start a search for the other companies in Orem. Then, I'd like to arrange for the sites that provided food to the rogue Tribanis to send their large transports here to collect a share of what we find."

The mayor looked at the other council members, who nodded "With a small share for this site?"

Ana smiled. "Of course."

Before she returned to London, Ana left Long in charge of finding the remaining companies in Salt Lake and Orem. She wanted to report the good news about the food stock to Phillip and the advisory council in person.

Prince Phillip and the advisory council were delighted at the quantity of preserved food available at the first company explored as this relieved their worries about running out of food. Ana then presented an unexpected proposal. She was concerned that the rogue Tribanis might discover the bad human food in one or more ships before all the ships were contaminated and return to take revenge on the Earth encampments. All the council members listed intently as she recommended combining encampments in several regions and restoring two or three ships in each region to be able to return to space and defend against the rogue ships should they return.

Based on her visits to 10 encampments so far, some were much further along establishing crops and a "normal" daily routine than others. She wanted to do a systematic evaluation of all encampments to see which could be closed and combined into those more thoroughly established. Expanding the fence around a combined encampment to allow more crops to be planted should be easy. The large transports of the restored transport ships could be used to move small buildings to a combined encampment.

At the end of her proposal, Paul assured her they would review the proposal.

Later, when they were alone, Phillip asked her why she was concerned about a possible return of the rogue group.

"You once said there was always a very small group of the non-leavers who were angry or envious of those leaving. What if there were some who did leave that really didn't want to leave and were angry their ancestors made that decision. Could they send a message to the rogue group that the food we gave is actually poisonous to them?"

Phillip stared at her for a moment. "Yes, it's possible. I don't think anyone here wishes to be back on Tribanus for many reasons, but what you are asking is certainly possible."

A few days later, Phillip and Ana met the advisory council to discuss how long it would take to make the changes Ana proposed. Paul said they had already sent a list of questions to each site mayor and based on the results it could all be accomplished in six months or less. Three ships could be restored for use in two months if necessary.

After some further discussion, the council agreed to begin combining encampments and restoring some ships for defensive purposes.

Chapter 40

NEW TEAMS

Captain Long met Ana when she arrived at the Houston encampment to discuss potential human leaders for the new negotiation teams. There were a number of Tribanis in the Houston Encampment who had known Ana since she was first brought there (in handcuffs) and were always eager to meet her now whenever she arrived. They had followed her successes leading the negotiations and were happy for her when she married their future king. Ana was shocked when she walked off the scout ship and dozens of Tribanis bowed and started cheering. Long stepped forward.

"Greetings, Your Highness. It seems there are a number of people who would like to meet you and thank you for your efforts in negotiating peace agreements with the various resistance movements."

Ana started shaking hands. Some she knew, others introduced themselves. It was a little overwhelming as Ana had never sought fame, only to avoid an awful conflict that no one would win.

In the conference room, she confided to Long that most of the humans she knew well were former members of the resistance group. Only a few names stood out as potential candidates, the leading candidate being Arun. She had given a list to Long in advance and she had arranged for several people on her list to be there for interviews.

Ana and Long met Arun first in the same conference room where she had first met Captain Morrison. It seemed strange for Long to be interviewing Arun to potentially lead a Tribani activity. Arun was excited at the idea and even suggested some other names for human team leads. Ana knew some of them but not all. She did think of asking about Camila and her boyfriend Robert. Arun said they had settled in a large house that sounded an awful lot like the house Sam had first shown her when she arrived looking for a new life. She wondered if Sam had suggested that house.

Arun volunteered to ask the people he had suggested, along with Camila and Robert to see if they would be interested. The interview ended and Long asked Arun to wait for her to finish the remaining interviews.

Ana and Long interviewed five more potential candidates for human team leads, then Long left Ana to discuss the team lead issue some more with Arun, and their own relationship of course.

Ana received an urgent video message from Paul in London. There had been some unauthorized communications from the Paris encampment to an unknown location. It had been encrypted but Paul assumed someone in that encampment was warning the rogue Tribanis of the contaminated food. Paul used a Tribani word that could translate to "traitor". Ana used the opportunity to ask Paul how long the trip from Tribanus to Earth took. He replied almost an Earth year. She remembered the Tribani historian saying that only Earth had enough water to sustain a large number of immigrants. She asked him if he had any idea where the rogue Tribanis could have built an enclosed city for as many as 200,000 immigrants (assuming 10000 per ship like their migration). Paul thought for a moment then displayed a star map and highlighted Tribanus, Earth and another planet that was known to have some water that appeared closer than Tribanus. She asked how long it would take if the rogue Tribanis returned from that planet to Earth. Paul guessed several months but he would get back to her with a more definitive answer.

Ana sat thinking. A few months would barely give them time to restore several ships to fight the rogue group if they returned immediately after receiving the transmission.

She returned to the more immediate problem of future negotiations. If three or four additional teams could be established, it would greatly accelerate the time to finish the negotiations and take a load off of her. She was also thinking about the possible reward for successful negotiations while avoiding a conflict.

Rogue Transmissions

To save some time, Ana contacted the mayors of all seventeen of the encampments in Europe and asked them to do the same thing the New York encampment had done (capture some representative humans around their encampments, tell them about the proposed peace negotiations, invite them to a meeting, and release them). This time she hoped they could do all the European sites together to save some time.

The strategy didn't work very well as only resistance groups near Paris and Munich Germany agreed to the negotiations. Ana would have to come up with something else for the rest.

George Adams, the mayor of the Paris encampment and Captain William Johnson, the site security leader (their English names) bowed when Ana walked out of the scout ship.

"Greeting, Your Highness. We are happy to finally meet you."

She shook their hands. "I have something we need to discuss that is more important than the peace negotiations."

Mayor Adams frowned. "Is there a problem?"

There were several Tribanis gathered around them who just wanted to meet Ana.

"We need to discuss this in private." She then turned and started meeting and greeting the Tribanis gathered around – almost like a politician running for office.

Once inside, she told them about the unauthorized transmissions from the Paris encampment and both were shocked. They knew about the contaminated food as the Paris encampment was one of the ten sites to transport food to the rogue Tribanis. They also had been informed they would be receiving specially prepared human food to replace their own stocks and were suitably skeptical as they had tried human food and found it to be inedible.

Mayor Adams was very unhappy that the transmissions had originated in the Paris encampment, but Captain Johnson was shocked. "Very few citizens or security personnel here have access to the transmission equipment. I know all of them and can't believe any one of them would do this."

"We are still trying to unscramble the transmissions, but they are well encrypted."

The mayor was emphatic "we will find those responsible and let the advisory council determine the appropriate punishment."

"The more important issue is the nature of the transmissions and will it lead to a return attack by the rogue group."

The mayor updated her on the plan to consolidate encampments. "There are only two encampments in the former country of France. We are planning on consolidating the other site to here, but it will take several months."

Ana nodded. "That seems to be typical for what we've heard so far."

Even though she was growing weary of the peace negotiations, she asked about the two resistance groups that agreed to meet.

The mayor showed a report from the seventeen sites that had asked local resistance groups to meet. So far only two had accepted. "One group is located near here, the other one will represent the resistance group located near Munich. As you requested, we notified them last night that we would meet them tomorrow. We will transport the Munich representative here in the morning. Both representatives can speak English."

"Did the advisory council notify you of possible negotiations in several Asian encampments?"

"Yes, so far, of the thirty sites that requested meetings with local groups, only three have accepted."

Ana shook her head and sighed. At this rate, there was no end in sight for peace agreement negotiations.

CHAPTER 41

EUROPEAN NEGOTIATIONS

The next day, a Tribani scout ship landed near the headquarters of the Paris encampment and the two designated resistance leaders were surprised when they were met by Captain Johnson and thoroughly searched for weapons even before they entered the encampment. Kurt Warner who represented the resistance movement in Munich Germany and Francoise Aucoin who represented a resistance group near Paris introduced themselves to Johnson.

Although Kurt and Francoise were supposed to be there to discuss a possible truce, their real mission was to find a way to kill as many Tribanis as possible and any human negotiators or die trying. They knew that would end any future attempt at a peace treaty. They were only vaguely aware of peace treaties agreed to in North America.

Captain Johnson led them to a conference room where Ana and five guards were waiting. Kurt and Tom were surprised at Anna's appearance. She was well dressed, slender, had a stylish hairdo and was wearing makeup. They both mentally compared her to the women in their own resistance movements. Kurt was thinking "She's pretty hot." Francoise was much younger and couldn't even remember when women looked like that. Both were surprised that she was introduced as a Tribani Princess.

After brief introductions, they all sat down, and Kurt and Tom were offered water. Ana began to go through her standard speech preceding discussion of the peace treaty proposal based on the agreements reached in North America. After a while she realized they were sizing up the guards and possible exits and were not paying attention to what she was saying. She suspected they were trying to figure out a way to attack her. She told the guards, in Tribani, to be on alert and they shifted their weapons to a ready state. Kurt and Tom knew they now had no chance of attacking Ana and sat back just staring at her. After a few minutes, Ana realized she was wasting her time.

"If you are not interested in a truce, then you can leave."

Warner almost yelled at her. "Why are you helping them?"

"What is the alternative?"

"Kill them all…" That surprised Captain Johnson who tightened his grip on his weapon. It didn't surprise Ana who suspected them of not being there in good faith.

"Then what? Do you have scientists or engineers that can restore power, or communications or even drinking water? Can you get the refineries running again and not have to rely on horses for transportation? If you did, your leaders would not have sent you to this meeting."

"So, we should just roll over and let them take over the Earth without a fight?"

"They did not come here to rule the Earth. Their sun was burning out and they had to leave if they wanted to survive. Earth happened to be the only planet they could travel to with a reasonable chance of survival."

She mentioned the effects of the meteor shower on the Tribanis as worse than for humans. She also told them they were not the source of the meteor shower.

That didn't seem to matter. "We don't care why they are here. We want them gone."

"Listen carefully to this. They no longer need a truce with Europe now or any other continent. North America has more land and resources than they will ever need. So, if you don't want an agreement, and continue attacking them, then they will move the seventeen settlements in Europe to North America and you will have won. But you should know that resistance movements like yours will no longer be needed so you can go back to being farmers or scavengers or pirates or whatever you were before they arrived."

Kurt and Francoise jumped up angrily and Kurt yelled. "You are a traitor."

Captain Johnson and the other guards were pointing their weapons at them, so they didn't make a move on Ana.

"You can call me whatever you like. In North America, power has been restored to the cities near many of the Tribani encampments and soon most of those areas will have clean running water again. If you don't want to face reality, then I hope you like your 19th century lives."

She motioned to the guards, and they escorted the representatives out.

Captain Johnson shook his head as they left. "That was an interesting encounter, Your Highness. I have never heard a human speak like this to another human."

"I've never spoken like that to any Tribani either. They were not sent here to negotiate a treaty, only to find a way kill all of us – probably to send a message that they will never negotiate."

The captain shook his head. "That is not what we want."

"I know that. Prince Phillip has made it clear many times that he wants to avoid a war if possible."

"What do you want to do now, Your Highness? Rest?"

"No, I'm okay – just frustrated. Could you contact the Asian negotiators and ask if we can meet them tomorrow?'

"Yes, immediately." He bowed slightly and left. Ana sat down and sighed.

Kurt and Francoise were interrogated by their leadership as soon as they returned to their own encampments. Their leaders were surprised, not that they failed to kill the Tribanis and Ana but the information she gave them about the North American agreements and that power and running water had been restored to some areas.

The Paris and Munich resistance leadership teams each held emergency meetings and voted to contact Ana again saying there had been a misunderstanding and that they really did wish to negotiate.

Ana received the messages with mixed feelings. She would have liked to establish treaties with these two sites but, then again, they had a chance and had blown it. She replied to each that she might be able to stop on the way back from the Asian summit.

Chapter 42

SECURITY LEAKS

When she returned to the Paris encampment, Mayor Adams and Captain Johnson held a confidential meeting with Ana regarding the unauthorized transmissions. Adams still seemed embarrassed that the transmission originated from his site. "We examined all the accesses to the transmission center at the time of the transmissions and have narrowed the possible personnel to two suspects."

Captain Johnson continued "we thought you would like to participate in our questioning of them."

"Oh, yes. It would really help if we knew what the messages said."

They led her to a conference room where a Tribani in a security uniform was waiting nervously. He jumped up and gave Captain Johnson the Tribani hand salute. He then bowed to Ana and Johnson told him to sit down. He was very young, and Ana doubted he was the culprit. Johnson and Adams took turns asking him questions until they told him he could leave.

Ana said what they were thinking. "I don't think he's the one."

A non-security communications specialist was interviewed next. He seemed to not be concerned about why he was even being questioned or the potential seriousness of the issue. Something seemed familiar about him to Ana, but she shrugged it off. How could she know anything about someone in the Paris encampment?

After two years of living with the Tribanis, Ana could now tell them apart not only by their looks but by their mannerisms and job functions. Most of the security men were very muscular but the security women were tall and slender (like Long). The communications specialist being interrogated reminded her of someone she saw or met in the London encampment. Then it came to her.

She interrupted Captain Johnson's questioning. "Did you have a relative in the London encampment that was killed in the same rocket attack that killed the queen?"

Johnson and Adams both looked at her in disbelief. How could she know that? They didn't know that she had a near total recall and the pictures of the dead were shown on the news and information channel for several days. This Tribani looked very much like one of the queen's aides.

The question also shocked the Tribani suspect. He stumbled on his answer, clearly lying and Ana knew he was responsible.

"What was the nature of your transmissions to the rogue Tribanis that came to Earth and demanded food and other items."

"I…don't know what you are talking about."

"Do you know the Tribani punishment for treason?" Ana didn't know but Paul had called him a traitor, so she threw that out to make him talk.

He was sweating now and squirming in his chair trying to find a way out of the interrogation room. He looked at Ana, then the mayor and captain and the two guards standing sentry by the door to the conference room. There was no way he was getting out of this.

Captain Johnson confronted him. "Your best chance of avoiding severe punishment is to tell us who you contacted and what exactly you told them."

He started slowly, then it seemed to gush out. He was angry that humans had killed his brother and sent several encrypted messages on a standard military band toward the planet that Paul had guessed earlier the rogue Tribanis had built their enclosed city.

"How did you know how to contact them?"

"I did not want to come to Earth. I had many friends in what you are calling the rogue group and wanted to go with them, but my brother convinced me to come to Earth with him. I was a communications specialist on Tribanus so contacting them was easy."

Ana had to know, "what did you tell them?"

"That the encampments are undefended, and humans have attacked many encampments, and the food given them was contaminated."

This was the worst case and Ana muttered "dammit" under her breath. She stood up and motioned the mayor and captain to follow her outside the conference room.

"If the consolidation were given the highest possible priority, how long would it take for you to have one ship ready to defend against the rogue group?"

The mayor and captain stared at each other for a moment, until the mayor replied. "With advisory council approval, we can have the ship ready in a few weeks – if we devote all our resources to it."

"Okay, assume you have approval. I'll contact Paul immediately."

Adams glanced back at the conference room door. "What about the traitor?"

"I'll ask Paul about that as well."

Johnson wondered aloud. "What about the Asian negotiations, set for tomorrow, Your Highness?"

"Let's continue on until we hear something different."

They both bowed and left to comply with her directions.

Ana immediately held a videoconference with Paul and Phillip to update them on the Paris negotiations and the uncovering of the traitor and his transmissions to the rogue group. They were both surprised and disappointed in the outcome of the meeting and the transmissions. Ana asked Paul and Phillip to discuss contacting all the encampments involved in the consolidations and giving them approval to place a high priority on getting ships ready to respond to a possible attack. Then she remembered the communications specialist.

"Is there a standard punishment for 'treason'?"

Paul and Phillip looked at each other, then Phillip replied. "It depends on the level of treason, from permanent banishment on a very remote location up to death, for the worst cases."

That reminded Ana of Phillip's initial offer to her of leading the peace negotiations or banishment. She thought it was ironic that some humans had called her a traitor. She thought about kicking Phillip in the leg when she returned.

Chapter 43

FUTURE OF NEGOTIATIONS

The next morning Ana and Captain Johnson met with the leaders of three resistance groups in Asia. She was disappointed that the results were similar to the brief European negotiations. When presented with the background of the Tribanis and the Romanis as the source of the meteor shower and then the North American standard conditions for a peace agreement (basically just stop all hostilities), the representatives from Beijing, Singapore and Hong Kong all rejected the terms. All said they would rather continue with their resistance efforts to force the Tribanis to leave. It didn't matter to them that the Tribanis were not responsible for the meteor shower. It was a short meeting and Ana and Captain Johnson were soon on the way back to the Paris encampment.

She didn't want to go back the advisory council with no positive results so before they left the Asian meeting site, she asked Captain Johnson to contact the resistance movements in Munich and Paris to arrange the meeting for a possible peace agreement.

This time, the leaders of those movements, not just their representatives, met with Ana and Captain Johnson and after a brief discussion of the terms, the leaders signed the treaty and promised to stop all hostilities.

On the way back to London, Ana struggled with how to address the remaining 15 European resistance movements near Tribani encampments that wouldn't even negotiate. And, what about the 30

Asian resistance movements that were still frequently attacking the encampments? She wondered if she would ever be able to end the negotiations.

When she arrived back in London, a rather large crowd of Tribanis were waiting to greet her. She was shocked that Phillip was there and had organized the crowd into a meeting line, as each wanted to shake her hand and thank her for her efforts to obtain peace agreements. It lifted her spirits after a few down days of failed negotiations.

Once she was alone the Phillip, he noticed she seemed upset.

"Do you remember the first time I saw you; you said I could either lead the peace negotiations or be sent to some far-off place where I would not be able to help the resistance?"

He stared for a moment, wondering why she asked. "Yes?"

"That's the same alternative offered to traitors."

She kicked him hard in the leg and he yelled. "Why did you do that?"

"That's for putting me on a par with traitors."

He was rubbing his leg as he replied. "I only said that assuming you would not choose the second choice. In my discussion with my father, we only wanted to ensure that you would lead the negotiations."

She was fuming, standing with her arms folded, when he limped over and put his arms around her. "I've missed being with you these last few days."

She slowly hugged him back. "Don't treat me like that again."

He laughed. "You have my word."

The next day, Ana and Phillip met with the advisory council to discuss future negotiations. Ana described future negotiations with the remaining resistance groups in Europe as "uncertain" at best and "bleak" in Asia. They clearly needed a new strategy. On a more positive note, Paul reported that four new negotiation teams had been created and were already starting to work with the remaining encampments in North America to set up meetings with local resistance movements. Ana was happy to see Arun leading the first team organized, along with Captain Long who volunteered to oversee his "security" at the meetings. She wondered how that would affect them personally. Being together all day, every day, can often make or break a relationship.

She was a little surprised that Camila and Robert had agreed to jointly lead a team. The remaining two teams were led by two of the people she and Long had interviewed. Now, she only had to figure out what to do about Europe and Asia. She assumed these new teams could also handle the seven encampments located on islands.

Paul also confirmed that a total of five existing encampments were being consolidated into other encampments with a high priority. This would allow their ships to be revamped for possible defense against the rogue group.

When that topic finished, Ana asked if she could discuss one possible way to solve the troubling negotiations issue.

"When we first met with the European representatives, it was clear they were not there to agree to a peace treaty. "

She then played a recording of part of the meeting.

> *"We don't care why they are here. We want them gone."*

> *"Listen carefully to this. They no longer need a truce with Europe now or any other continent. North America has more land and resources than they will ever need. So, if you don't want an agreement, and continue attacking them, then they will move the seventeen settlements in Europe to North America and you will have won. But you should know that resistance movements like yours will no longer be needed so you can go back to being farmers or*

scavengers or pirates or whatever you were before they arrived."

When she stopped the recording, she saw the shocked expressions on everyone's face.

"I was angry and said that without thinking about it. But after some reflection, I was wondering if that wouldn't be one possible solution to the Europe and Asia problem. What if we consolidated the European and Asian encampments that won't negotiate into the 25 in North America, or some new sites and let the resistance movements in those areas just fade away. There is plenty of land and resources for all Tribanis in North America."

There was a stunned silence. Most of the advisory council members, including Phillip were too shocked to reply.

"Look, this is just one possibility for solving the peace negotiation problems with resistance groups that aren't interested. I'm open to your possibilities."

Paul finally answered. "This is a very difficult solution to the problem."

Ana was not deterred. "Difficult, but not impossible. What if you didn't have to worry about constant attacks. Isn't that worth the effort?"

Blake Eades was the council's security focal point, and all the site security focal points reported to him. "I think this is an excellent idea, fewer sites would be much easier to defend, and we could adjust our forces to meet local security needs."

James Bennett, the cultural focal point, was not supportive. "This looks like we are not capable of defending ourselves. Our people would ask why we are being pushed out of most areas and, essentially, giving up to the actions of the resistance."

That one was more difficult, but Ana had an answer. "Most Tribanis want to get on with their lives, whether that's in North America, or Europe or Asia, they probably don't care."

Phillip agreed. "I will discuss this possibility with my father. Let me know if there are any viable alternatives to the European and Asia negotiations." He got up to leave and all the council members rose and bowed. Ana noticed they were all now looking at her.

"What?"

Before anyone could answer, a large video screen in the room came on with an urgent message from the Paris encampment. Mayor Adams appeared. "I am sorry to interrupt your meeting, but we have just received an unauthorized transmission that was probably intended for the communications specialist who contacted the rogue group."

Paul looked worried. "Were you able to break the code?"

Adams nodded and read the transmission to the council. "Your information was received too late. All transports were infected by the contaminated food. We have been unable to contain the organisms and fear our own planet may now be infected as well. We have sent your message to the Romanis inviting them to now proceed with their efforts to establish an outpost on Earth, since the current encampments are undefended and currently being attacked by humans."

There were several audible gasps in the room. Ana looked at Paul, "That the species you came in contact with that were intending to colonize Earth and you fought the war with?"

"Yes. This is the worst thing the rogue group could possibly do. Now this species knows we have no defense against attacks from space, and that some humans survived."

Ana sat thinking while one of the council members went to bring Phillip back to the meeting. Paul seemed to be lost in thought, but she asked him "do you know how far the Romanis home planet is? How long will it take for them to come here?"

He shook his head. "Not long I'm afraid. Certainly not long enough to restore our ships to be able to defend us." He saw Ana smile. "What are you thinking?" By now, Paul and most of the council respected Ana's ideas and suggestions, even if they didn't always agree with them.

"Instead of fighting them, why not invite them to come?"

Most of the council members looked at each other in shock. Paul frowned. "What do you mean?"

"We could pretend to be the communications specialist in Paris and send them a map showing all the encampments in Europe, except for Paris and Munich, and all the sites in Asia, under the pretense of showing them where the undefended sites are. Then, evacuate those sites before they arrive, remove the perimeter fences, and notify the local resistance groups that the sites have been abandoned."

Paul slowly smiled. "You would use local resistance groups to fight the Romanis?"

"Yes. But we need to get a few ships back in service and into space to warn us when they are coming so we know when to evacuate."

Prince Phillip returned to the meeting as Ana was describing her plan to defend against the new alien species. He laughed, and all the council members rose and bowed to him.

"Another interesting plan. How do you come up with them?"

"I only offer possibilities."

Paul addressed the council. "Are there any other possible alternatives?"

No one volunteered any, so Paul asked Phillip. "If you agree, we will start on this immediately."

"I think I can speak for the king. If there is no other possibility developed in the next day or so, we should proceed. My father agreed with the plan to combine encampments to free up migration ships to defend against the rogue Tribanis. I will discuss the idea of moving encampments from Europe and Asia and inviting the Romanis to former sites. Let's assume we will continue with that plan until the Romanis arrive unless an alternative is developed. We only need to develop an evacuation plan in case they arrive before the sites are moved."

Ana commented. "We could use each site's large transport for an emergency evacuation and the evacuees could live in the encampment ships in North America until they can be relocated permanently."

Paul nodded and then asked each council member for plan input, in their area of expertise.

The next several months seemed to fly by for Ana. She became the focal point for coordinating the evacuation of most of the landing sites in Europe and all of Asia. The other peace negotiation teams had obtained agreements for the rest of the North American sites and the African sites and were now working with the South America encampments to facilitate peace agreements. The North American sites, now free of a constant threat of attack had already expanded their encampments with fence components and small buildings transported from Europe and Asia. They still needed electronic fences to keep out the wild animals. A few sites in Europe and Asia were now abandoned and the local resistance groups moved in to occupy what was left behind. Some of the resistance groups had already disbanded and returned to whatever they were doing to survive before the Tribanis arrived.

Ana was in a meeting with the advisory council when an urgent message arrived from the captain of one of the Tribani ships that had returned to space. A large armada of ships was approaching, and from intercepted communications between them, the Tribani captain confirmed they were Romanis. Based on their speed and distance, they would arrive in less than two weeks. Paul confirmed the details then addressed the council.

"We need to start immediate evacuations of the remaining target sites. If there is time left, we can take as much equipment as possible until they arrive."

There was one last council meeting just before the Romanis arrived. Paul provided an update.

"All the target sites have been evacuated. Most of the fences and buildings have been recovered and moved to sites in North America. All we can do now is wait."

Ana wondered if their preparation would be adequate. "How many ships will be available to fight the Romanis once they land?"

"More than fifty."

Ana pulled Paul aside from the other council members. "I thought the Romanis were not colonizers, but raiders that took what they needed and proceeded to their next conquest?"

Paul nodded. "That was our understanding. Why are you asking about them now?"

"I heard the meteor shower chemical would affect them even more than humans. So, they must be here only to attack and take what they need for their future raids."

"Yes, we don't expect them to build anything permanent."

Ana just shook her head. "What a waste of people and resources."

Paul nodded.

Forty Romani ships landed without incident in the former Tribani sites in Europe and Asia. They immediately knew something was wrong when they encountered no Tribani resistance and found the remains of the base encampments. They were caught off guard when they were immediately attacked from the ground by local resistance groups whenever they ventured outside their ships, and by Tribani ships from space. A few Romani ships were able to take off and each time, they were attacked and destroyed by superior numbers of Tribani ships. The whole conflict lasted only two days before the Romanis realized they had no chance to win and contacted the Tribanis to agree on an exit plan from Earth.

Phillip held a videoconference with the leader of the Romanis to discuss her exit plan but explained that there wasn't anything he could do about the local resistance groups as they had been unable to reach a peace type agreement with them.

The Romani leader asked what they could do to stop the local attacks, and Phillip said to "leave" or fight them.

Ana asked Phillip to ask the Romani leader how they hoped to survive on Earth. Micro-organisms in the air, water and soil could be deadly without some form of protection. The leader replied they hoped to live in their ships and wear protective suits until they collected the food and water they needed. Phillip saw Ana smile.

"What are you thinking."

"Unlike some planets they have attacked, Earth biosphere is so complex it's unlikely they will ever collect any food or water that won't sicken or even kill them." She Laughed. "Perhaps we could give them some special human food, like the kind we gave the rogue Tribanis – as a gift of course."

Phillip laughed. "Another excellent suggestion. I'll ask the advisory council to coordinate that if they agree."

Ana was smiling and Philip suspected there was something she was not telling him. "What are you smiling about?"

"Even the prepper food will probably kill them. Cooking will kill most bacteria but there are other organisms that will survive and the Romanis will have no natural defense against them." She thought a minute. "The purified water might be okay, but even then, there could be minerals or other trace elements that could harm them. But they are pirates, so what do they expect?"

Phillip laughed then contacted the Romani leader with the offer of some human food and purified water if they would leave immediately and the Romani leader replied by asking if the Tribanis would let them leave peacefully if they accepted the water and food gifts. Phillip said they could leave but only one ship at a time and that ship would be escorted away from Earth to keep them from returning and attacking.

They both agreed to communicate with their leaders and work on the details of the plan if it was agreed to, and then communicate again when they had a resolution.

Chapter 44

ROGUE TRIBANIS

Just like any other day, Ana left Phillip to discuss issues with his father and headed for the advisory council building, when she was confronted by three aliens in protective suits. She thought about trying to run away, but they were pointing weapons at her.

"What do you want?"

The apparent leader replied in Tribani. "Are you Ana?"

"Yes?"

"Come with us."

"Who are you?"

"It doesn't matter, you will come with us."

They led her to a small scout ship, but Ana immediately knew it was not the same as their scout ships. This was a rogue Tribani group's scout ship.

"I can't go in there, the micro-organisms in the air will kill me."

One of the three rogue Tribanis contacted their leader, then turned to her.

"We have sterilized one section so you will not be harmed." He motioned her to board the ship.

As soon as she entered the ship, she recognized the rogue Tribani leader waiting for her. She was surprised he wasn't wearing a protective suit. He motioned her to follow him to a small meeting room and to a seat at a table. He sat down opposite her.

"I have heard a lot about you Ana Cordoba."

"You shouldn't believe everything you hear."

He laughed. "Your Tribani is excellent. By the way, my name is Rokkus. I was chosen to lead by those who wished to leave Tribanus but did not want to be subjects of the person who calls himself King Henry."

He looked exactly the same as in the video meetings with Phillip. In person, he looked even more ominous. She tried to remain calm, as she knew the best defense is often a good offense.

"What do you want with me?"

"We know you are somehow responsible for including the bad human food in with the Tribani food we received."

Ana was surprised. The Tribani "traitor" in Paris was in custody and could not have revealed that information to him. Was there another traitor communicating with the rogue group?

"Who told you that?"

"It doesn't matter. We are going to trade you for the food Phillip promised, but this time without the poisonous human food."

"Why would Phillip trade that much food to you, for me?"

"We don't understand human customs, but we know you have some sort of personal relationship with Phillip, and we believe he will make this trade."

"And if he doesn't?"

"We will take you back to our new city with us."

"You know the micro-organisms and bacteria in a Tribani city will kill me in a very short time."

From his expression and the tone of his voice she guessed he was becoming angry. "The same as your poisonous food organisms has killed many of us."

"You came here to take what you want. We gave you that and a little more. You even just threatened to kidnap me if you don't get what you want."

She could tell he was still angry, but seemed to be calming down, so she decided to change the subject. She thought she knew the answer to her next question, but she wanted to hear him say it. "Why didn't you plan better and bring enough food with you?"

"We did, but unfortunately the soil of the planet is incompatible with the plants we brought with us. Once the Tribani soil they are in is no longer useful, we will have no food."

That was a different answer than she expected. "I thought all food on Tribanus has been grown in containers of soil in the cities for a very long time."

"Yes, but there is a large cache of fresh Tribani soil in each city for future plantings. It is well-guarded, and we could not bring significant quantities of that soil with us."

"So, how does receiving the food and plants you want from Phillip, solve that problem?"

"It will give us needed time to find a way to modify the plants so they will grow in the planet's soil."

"No, it won't. The agricultural expert on the king's Advisory Council told me the plants they brought with them have been slowly modified over a very long time, so they would be compatible with the soil on Earth. Those plants would not survive in the soil of your new planet, either. Even with the plants from Phillip, you will not have enough food to survive long enough to modify them."

Rokkus just stared at her. The immensity of the problem he faced was now evident.

Ana thought they could use some help with hydroponics. "What if I could help you make your Tribani soil productive again?"

Ana almost laughed at the skepticism on his face as her fear of him had faded.

"Even if that were possible, why would you help us?"

"You mentioned a trade. What would you give me, if I could help you restore the soil you brought with you?"

He was shocked when he realized she was now negotiating with him. "What do you want?"

"The Romanis are here because you told them encampments on Earth were unprotected."

"Yes?"

"It appears they plan on killing all humans near the sites wherever they land. We want them gone." She realized she now sounded like Arun the first time they met.

"What do you want us to do?"

"Convince them to leave, somehow. Do whatever you need to do."

"Most of our ships were contaminated by the poisonous human food, and we are still trying to recover. We have limited means to force the Romanis to leave."

"Then you'll have to come up with another way."

Rokkus was rubbing his chin while he thought about the deal. Ana realized that Phillip had the same unconscious habit whenever he was trying to figure out a forward plan. She wondered if that was an individual trait or possibly cultural.

"If I agree to this, how do I know you can help restore the soil?"

"Farmers on Earth used to know how to restore their fields by changing the crops they planted and using fertilizers that provide nutrients that help a plant grow faster and bigger and produce more food. I'm sure we can find some fertilizers that will help. I'll discuss it with the agricultural expert on the Advisory Council."

"All right. When do you want to meet again to discuss how this agreement is working?"

"Give me a week or so."

"A week?"

"That's seven days or rotations of the Earth. I heard Phillip say 20 sones is about 30 hours on Earth, so that's a little more than 110 sones. Contact Phillip again in about 120 sones."

When she stood up, Rokkus stood as well.

"What exactly is your relationship with Phillip?"

"We're married. I'll let you figure out what that means."

Rokkus frowned but instructed the guards to take her back to where they found her.

Chapter 45

FERTILIZERS

Phillip was angry that it had been so easy to abduct Ana. Why didn't they detect a rogue scout ship landing inside the London encampment? He ordered an immediate review of all communications and security systems. Ana had gone straight to Phillip about the encounter as she was concerned the potential traitor giving sensitive information to the rogue group was in the London site. She didn't even trust the Advisory Council, as she only knew a few well enough to eliminate them as the possible source of leaks. Phillip had known most of the council members for a long time and it was difficult for him to believe any one of them could be the traitor.

Phillip trusted Paul Mainer enough to include him in the discussion on what to do next. He was as shocked as Phillip that someone in the encampment could be in contact with the rogue group. He personally checked all incoming and outgoing transmissions for destination. All sites were allowed to transmit messages back to Tribanus for various reasons. Some personal transmissions back to relatives on Tribanis were even allowed on a very limited basis. Paul recruited a team of technicians he trusted who helped him check transmissions between encampments, as there were many of these compared to the limited number of transmissions back to Tribanus.

Almost all Tribanis on Earth knew who Ana was, based on the broadcast of her marriage to Phillip. However, very few would have known her role in adding spoiled human food to the food shipments to the rogue group. Captain Long had personally coordinated the delivery of the human food hidden inside Tribani food containers to the other encampments and told those encampments it was something the rogue group had requested, that only the London site could provide. She had reported back that there were no questions or concerns at any site when she delivered the "special" food.

While all that was going on, Ana met with the agricultural focal point on the council (after Paul personally cleared her) about adding fertilizers to Tribani soil to restore its usefulness. She understood what Ana was telling her, but they didn't have anything that would solve the problem.

Ana wasn't familiar with the distribution of fertilizers in the former UK, so she traveled to Houston and met Captain Long and Arun to talk about fertilizers. They were surprised at first as Ana described her encounter with Rokkus, but then eager to help her if possible. After meeting several of his former resistance members, Arun marked the location of several potential farm hardware stores that might have some types of fertilizer, on an aerial survey map.

While studying the map, Ana remembered the farm hardware store where Sam found the diesel generator and they visited that store first. There were several types of fertilizers in large plastic bags in a large warehouse behind the store. Ana wasn't an expert in fertilizers, so Captain Long arranged for several large bags of each type to be transported back to London.

With the agricultural expert's help, they added small amounts of different fertilizers to several Tribani soil samples that appeared to be no longer useful. They added some small plants and seeds to each sample and watered them. Ana reasoned that if this worked for the plants that had been modified to grow on Earth, it should work for the original plants the rogue group brought to their new planet. Now, all they had to do was wait.

Rokkus contacted Phillip a week after his encounter with Ana. Phillip went first and described their progress with fertilizers. Phillip was more concerned about the rogue group's progress in getting the Romanis to leave Earth.

"And what progress is being made in getting the Romanis to leave Earth?"

Rokkus laughed. "We sent them a message that appeared to come from their home planet that they are being attacked by ships from Tribanus and ordering them to return and defend it. They replied that they are being attacked on Earth by humans and Tribanis whenever they leave Earth. They now seem desperate to leave and will probably be contacting you to speed up the negotiations to leave."

The next day, the Romanis did contact Phillip to try and speed up their departure from Earth. Since Ana was now the de facto negotiator for the Tribanis, Phillip asked her to work out a plan to ensure the Romanis left as soon as possible.

She met the Romani leader via teleconference and was surprised that she was about the same size as her with a green skin color, black hair and large black eyes. She was also wearing a military type uniform. The Romani leader seemed surprised that Ana was leading the negotiations, as she was expecting to see a Tribani in that role, probably Phillip or Paul. When she said that, Ana wondered how she knew who Phillip and Paul were. Was the apparent traitor who communicated with the rogue Tribanis also in contact with the Romanis?

After some negotiations, all the senior Romani leaders on Earth agreed to be held by the Tribanis until all the Romanis ships were gone and not likely to re-group, return and attack the Tribani encampments.

Phillip and the Advisory Council agreed and as soon as Ana confirmed the deal, a large Tribani security team in protective clothing landed near the Romani leader's ship and entered it, taking her and the other Romani leaders into custody. Soon, the Romani ships started leaving individually for their home planet. When they were out of the solar system, the last ship with the Romani leaders was allowed to leave.

Ana held another meeting with Rokkus and informed him that a combination of several fertilizers had seemingly restored the exhausted Tribani soil, and the plants were now growing in it. Based on the results, Captain Long transported a large supply of fertilizer to the London encampment. Rokkus' ship was allowed to land in the London encampment and the large cache of fertilizer bags were transferred to it. He held one final meeting with Phillip and Ana thanking them for helping them survive on their new planet. He even described negotiations underway with a number of governments on Tribanus to build several more enclosed cities on the new planet for a growing number of Tribanis who wished to risk the move there, as life outside their enclosed cities was now impossible, and life inside was becoming difficult. All remaining Tribanis knew they could not migrate to Earth because of the bacteria and micro-organisms, and the long time required for DNA modifications to be compatible.

Before she left, Long handed Ana another note from Sam. She commented as Ana read the note. "He doesn't have a communicator or a tablet…"

Sam had successfully installed all five of the transporter power packs into two small cars, a light pickup truck, a motorcycle and even a boat. He was asking if he could receive a large number of the transporter power packs to continue his conversions as other former resistance groups had heard about his work and were offering to trade all kinds of valuable items for a converted car or truck.

Ana smiled, she could imagine Sam starting a business and becoming pretty well off with his conversions. She thought about her own personal situation with Phillip and decided to send Paul Mainer a request for 110 power packs for Sam. Her request included a justification of helping former resistance groups improve their transportation ability by allocating two units per site for the 55 sites that already signed or agreed to sign a peace agreement.

Sam had helped her when she needed it. It was the least she could do.

Chapter 46

SECURITY ISSUES

Ana and Paul became determined to find the person responsible for communicating to the rogue group and possibly the Romanis, information that was harmful to their security.

They naturally started with the communications expert on the advisory council. Ana remembered the door leading to the communications or computer equipment at the Houston encampment. Ana still remembered it because it was one of the few guarded doors in the whole encampment. Why was it guarded? A quick trip to the communications center in the London encampment confirmed it was guarded as well.

Paul and Ana held a private meeting with James Harris, the council security advisor. Ana began the questioning.

"When I was in the Houston encampment, I noticed there were very few doors that were guarded, out of possibly thousands of doors. There is also a guard at the communications center here. Why are the communications centers guarded?"

James had no idea about the purpose of the meeting, and it was clear he was not expecting that question.

"Shortly after we landed on Earth, there were several unauthorized transmissions made from several transport ships. We couldn't determine the destination and they were encrypted. Transmissions back to Tribanus are scheduled and controlled to ensure everyone who wants to communicate has an opportunity to do so. After we found out about the unauthorized transmissions, we tightened access and increased security at each communication center."

Paul was shocked. "Why didn't you inform the advisory council of this?"

"There have been no additional unauthorized communications, we still don't know who was involved, or the nature of the transmissions or their destinations. I wanted to wait until we had something to report."

Ana was more concerned about the present. "Are you sure this has not happened recently? The rogue Tribanis led by Rokkus knew I was responsible for adding the spoiled human food to the Tribani food they forced us to give them. This was many months after you landed on Earth."

Harris was not aware that Rokkus knew Ana had been involved. He shook his head. "It's not possible. We keep detailed transmission logs. I would know if this happened."

"Did you know that the communications specialist in Paris informed the rogue Tribanis and the Romanis that some humans had survived and were attacking Tribani encampments?"

Harris was shocked, and it showed. "No."

"Could there be other communication specialists involved? Could the logs be modified so that there are no records of the transmissions?"

Harris shook his head. "I know most of them. It's very unlikely they would do this or modify the logs."

Paul was determined to find out how these communications happened. "Set up a team to examine the logs and talk to every communications specialist. Use whatever means is necessary to ensure they are not covering up these activities."

Harris grimaced. "Yes, sir."

When Harris left, Ana asked Paul "do you use lie detectors?"

Paul frowned. "Lie detectors?"

"Machines that can used to determine whether someone is telling the truth or lying. There are also some chemicals that inhibit someone from lying when they are questioned."

Paul shook his head. "We don't have anything like that."

"I'll see if I can find something and let you know."

Ana hadn't seen Captain Long in a while, so she asked her to meet her in New York City the next day. Ana had kept in contact with several former resistance leaders in New York. Two of them seemed very friendly and eager to get the power back on to a much larger area around New York, as soon as possible. She contacted James and Bill to see if they knew of any museum that might have a lie detector that could be resurrected. By now, power had been restored to large portions of New York and it would be possible to test the detector on a suitable subject. A day later James replied they found one and sent location directions to the Spyscaper Museum to Ana.

Although resistance in the New York area had largely stopped, Long didn't want to take a chance on Ana being harmed and had a small security detail escort them to the museum. A few guards waited outside while others followed Ana and Long to a small room in the back of the museum.

James and Bill immediately led them to a small room in the museum where they showed her a lie detector with a manual. They had placed it on a table and moved to the back when Ana and Long entered. Ana noticed the local resistance leaders staring at Long. They had seen a number of muscular male Tribani security guards and were surprised that Long was tall and slender. She was also wearing her silver captain's uniform with a blue collar and several blue stripes on the sleeves.

James whispered to Ana. "Do all Tribani females look like her?"

Ana laughed. "Most of them." When she looked closer at Long, she noticed subtle changes. Her blond hair was longer now and had a few curls and she was even wearing a small amount of makeup. Was she wearing perfume? She would ask her about that later.

Long didn't have a clue what was going on but volunteered to help. She looked around to make sure the Tribanis guards were not in the room.

"What are we doing, Ana?"

She pointed to the wooden box on a table in front of them. "That's a lie detector. We want to see if it will work on Tribanis as well as humans."

"Lie detector? What is a lie?"

"That's when someone says something that they know isn't true."

Long looked surprised and shook her head. "I don't do that."

"I'm not saying you do; I just want to see if this machine still works. We first need to attach some leads to you." She motioned Long to sit down at the table and James and Bill attached six electrodes to her.

"Will this hurt?"

"You won't feel a thing."

"What do you want me to do?"

"I'll ask you a series of questions and on one of them, make up an answer but don't tell me which one. We'll start in English and then I'll ask the same questions in Tribani. Make sure you make up the answer to the same question."

Long nodded and Ana began by asking her simple questions like her name and age to establish a baseline.

What's your name?"

"Captain Sarah Long."

"How old are you?"

Long thought about that for a moment. "Two years."

Ana, James and Bill laughed.

"Ok, how old were you when you left Tribanus?"

"Almost 146000 sones."

Ana saw the former resistance leaders frown. "They don't mark years." She did some quick math on the lie detector paper. "That's about 25 years."

Long nodded as Bill whispered to Ana. "Their birthday cakes must be huge."

Ana smiled and then asked the rest of her questions, marking the question number on the paper chart next to Long's responses. One of the questions related to the origin of the meteor shower and Long replied that the Romanis were responsible. Ana noted on the chart that her response was truthful. She then repeated the same questions in Tribani, also marking the question numbers on the chart.

When it was done, James and Bill gently removed the electrodes, and they gathered around the machine.

"I think you made up the answer to "Do you miss Tribanus, and you said 'yes'. Is that the false answer?"

"Yes, I never think about Tribanus. There is so much going on here and I like to focus on the future, not the past."

Ana compared that question's answer with the same question asked in Tribani and the response was the same.

"This looks promising, I'll tell Paul immediately."

Long left to contact the scout ship for their return. The lie detector box had a top with a handle and Bill closed the box and handed it to Ana.

"Did you find some extra rolls of paper and ink for the pens?"

"Yes, we spent hours in the museum storage area, but we finally found a few rolls and some ink." He handed her a small box with several rolls of paper and a bottle of ink. "You owe me one for this."

Ana laughed. "What do you want?"

"Does Captain Long have a boyfriend?"

Ana smiled. "Yes, she actually has a human fiancé."

"Darn. Does she have any girlfriends?"

"I'm sure she does. Why don't you ask her?"

"How would I do that?"

During peace negotiations, each resistance leader was given a communicator in case they had additional questions or wanted more information. Ana noticed that Bill and James had added a belt clip to their communicators. She motioned to Bill to give her his communicator. When he handed it over, Ana entered a series of numbers then handed it back.

"Communicators can also call each other. That's Captain Long's number. Please don't share it. Just wait a while and ask her about her friends."

Bill stared at a number displayed on the communicator. "I thought these could only contact your group…thanks."

On the way back to the transport, Ana filled Long in on the possible traitors in the communications areas that led to the rogue Tribanis visit and demands for food and other supplies and the communications that led the Romanis to attack. Long was shocked but now she understood why Ana wanted to use the lie detector to find out the truth.

"To change the subject…have you changed your hair?"

Long blushed. "Yes. Arun likes it this way."

"Are you wearing some makeup?"

"Yes, Arun likes it."

"And are you wearing perfume?"

Long blushed again. "Yes, Arun likes this one."

"Why are you trying so hard to please him?"

"When I do what he likes, he makes a big effort to do what I like." She then said a word in Tribani that roughly translated to 'oral sex'.

Ana laughed. "I'll leave it at that." She paused. "By the way, you made quite an impression on James and especially Bill."

"Impression?"

"They wanted to know more about you, even if you were in a relationship."

Long laughed.

"I told them you had a fiancé, but they then wanted to know if you had any female friends who weren't in a relationship."

"Is this true?"

"Yes, I'm sure they were serious. They may give you a call…"

Long chuckled. Bill was kind of cute. "I have a few friends that may be interested."

As they neared the ship, Ana asked "how is your relationship with Arun?"

"I have decided to marry him."

"Have you told him?"

"I plan to do that when I return to Houston."

"I would be happy to be your Maid of Honor."

"That would be a great honor, Ana."

"Just let me know when you set a date."

Long smiled at the formality of marriage compared to the informal permanent relationship most Tribanis still agreed to.

When Ana returned to London, she and Phillip spent the night 'catching up'. The next morning, she saw an announcement on her tablet that Dr Barry Sailfish had been promoted to Chief Health Officer for all the North American encampments. She sent him a message congratulating him on his promotion and then suddenly remembered his forwarded message from the female health specialist in London about the lower probability of conception for humans and Tribanis. She found the specialist's contact information and messaged her asking if there was anything that could be done to improve the likelihood of conception.

The female health specialist was shocked to receive a message from the princess and answered immediately. Ana was surprised that the health specialist replied so quickly that in two more Tribani generations the probability of conception would be much higher, not all that different than the problems/issues human couples occasionally encounter. She also had a recommendation that a male Tribani partner drink a special mixture of ingredients that were known to greatly enhance sperm production and motility, effectively overwhelming the egg. She even offered to obtain the necessary ingredients and send the mixture to Ana. Ana replied that she was grateful for the help, and asked how soon she could supply the drink.

She also wondered how Phillip would react when she asked him to drink a special mixture to improve their chances of contraception. To her surprise, Phillip was enthusiastic and when given the first sample to drink, downed it eagerly. Ana smiled.

The next day, Ana met Paul and security focal point James Harris to discuss using the lie detector. Ana suggested they begin with the lead communication specialist in London.

George Barnes had no clue as to why he was being summoned to meet with James Harris. Harris was on the Advisory Council and reported to Prince Phillip. He was at least three levels higher than his own supervisor. What did he want? When he entered the conference room, he was shocked to see the princess, the head of the Advisory Council, and his own supervisor in addition to Harris.

Harris told him where to sit. He couldn't help but notice the small wooden box on the table in front of him.

There was a general agreement the questioning would be done in Tribani so there wouldn't be a mistaken answer due to a language error. Harris began the meeting.

"George Barnes, we have been concerned that someone or a group of people have been trying to undermine our activities on Earth by communicating with other species who are not friendly or are even our enemies. We want to ask you some questions, but we are going to try an experimental procedure that humans use to judge the validity of your answers – with that box in front of you."

Barnes almost passed out when two security guards he hadn't even noticed started connecting electrodes to him.

Harris tried to calm him. "This won't hurt."

Ana gave Harris a list of questions as a starting point. She said they could add more depending on Barnes' answers.

It seemed like a dream, but the princess was seated across the table from him and started writing on a piece of paper that was moving through the machine. Six pens were writing on the paper and making small wiggly lines. Harris got his attention then started asking several "baseline" questions. He calmed down a little when Harris asked his name and age (which he gave in sones). Ana made a quick calculation that Barnes was about 30 years old. After a few more baseline type questions of where he worked and who was his supervisor, Harris then asked him if he had ever made any communications that were not authorized or recorded in the communications log. Barnes tried hard to remain calm and replied that he had never done anything like that.

Ana was writing the question numbers on the machine's chart and circled Barnes' last answer where the pen needles were now making large marks on the chart.

"I'm afraid this device says you are not telling the truth."

Barnes almost passed out. "It must be wrong. I am telling the truth."

Ana interrupted Harris' line of questions with a quick follow-up. "Were you the one who contacted the Romanis telling them humans were attacking the base camps and the camps were mostly undefended?"

Barnes instinctively answered before thinking. "No, it was Tom Akers." He gasped when he realized what he had admitted and put his hands over his mouth.

Ana looked at the chart, then at the others in the room. "By the way, that was a true statement."

Harris was also seated across from Barnes who was now staring off into space while considering the consequences of his actions. Harris picked up the writing device Ana had put down and tapped on the table to get Barnes' attention.

"George Barnes, you know the penalty for high treason. Your only hope to avoid that punishment is to help us find all the others who are committing these actions which are undermining our safety and security."

Barnes was visibly shaking when he looked at him. "What do you want to know?"

"The names of the others in the group, how they are hiding these transmissions and any other transmissions we don't know about that may also threaten us."

Ana and Paul left the meeting to Harris and Barnes supervisor, when the details of how the transmissions were hidden were described, as it was fairly technical. She was only interested that they could break that process and uncover all past rogue transmissions.

Barnes basically admitted that he was a part of a group of disaffected Tribanis who really didn't want to migrate to Earth but felt they had no choice since their DNA was now almost human.

Harris quickly determined the process to hide their efforts was a combination of communication channels that were never used by the Tribanis, the communications were encrypted by keys that were constantly changed and the transmissions were often done during the night. If a communication were somehow recorded, the members quickly deleted it before it became a permanent record in the log.

As the questioning continued, Harris and Barnes' supervisor were dismayed that these rogue communicators had even contacted a warrior-like species near the center of the galaxy. In exchange for detailed information about Earth and the Tribani settlements, they asked to be spared and leave them in charge once they conquered all Tribani settlements.

So far there had been no reply, which could be a good thing or a bad thing.

Barnes was taken to a holding cell and Harris left to coordinate the arrest and jailing of all the other members of the conspiracy. In the meantime, Harris filled in the advisory council with their findings to determine a plan going forward. Paul summarized what they knew about the warrior species. They had run into them early in the search for a new home, but that species was already engaged in a full-blown war with another species near the center of the galaxy and pretty much ignored them. In their communications with other species during the search, the warrior species was well known and thought to be impossible to negotiate with. Although their weapons were not superior, they employed a "bum rush" strategy of overwhelming their enemies with vast numbers of ships and warriors. Luckily, Earth was in a relatively remote area of the galaxy and the warrior species was not interested in such a remote area – so far.

Chapter 47

ROMANI ISSUES

Just when it appeared the threats from the rogue Tribanis and the Romanis had finally been resolved, the leader of the rogue Tribanis, Rokkus, contacted Ana again with an urgent request for a video meeting. She agreed and soon was staring at Rokkus again on a video screen.

"What happened? Did the fertilizers not restore the spent Tribani soil for Madjuul plants?"

"No, that is working, but we just received word the Romanis found out we were behind the false transmission that Tribanus was attacking Romanus, that caused them to leave Earth before they could gather the water and food they needed. They are threatening to attack our new city."

"So, why are you contacting us?"

"We need your help. If we could combine our ships with your ships that attacked the Romani sites on Earth, we could defeat them and end their threat."

"You don't have anything to worry about."

Rokkus seemed confused. "What do you mean?"

"The Tribani food we 'gifted' to encourage them to leave also contained some past its prime human food, much like we gave you."

Rokkus was shocked. "What?"

"It won't take long for them to suffer the same fate your people encountered with the questionable food."

Rokkus was thoughtful for a moment. "That food caused severe problems for us. If they don't figure it out quickly, it could completely destroy them."

Ana shrugged but didn't say anything.

"Are you not concerned that you may have just wiped out an entire species?"

"They came to take what they wanted. We gave them something extra. I think they got what they deserved."

Rokkus laughed as he had heard Ana say almost the same thing about his own efforts to take Tribani food from Earth. "We are fortunate to now have a truce with you."

"There is plenty of room on Earth if you decide to modify your DNA and become human. If you do, contact us in 60 generations or so and we will give you some landing site locations."

Rokkus started to laugh, then stopped. "Are you serious?"

"I'll let you figure that out." She waved to him and disconnected.

Rokkus sat thinking for a while. Was she serious? Should he bring this up at the next Leadership Council meeting and discuss it? He decided to tell the council about the hazardous food given to the Romanis and, if it seemed appropriate, bring up the DNA modification plan.

Chapter 48

LONG AND ARUN

Now that the immediate threat of the Romanis was gone and most encampments had finalized agreements with local resistance groups, there wasn't much that required immediate action from Ana and Phillip, they jointly decided to finish their honeymoon in Hawaii that was originally cut short by the arrival of the rogue Tribani group.

This time, soon after they returned Ana knew something had happened when she threw up the next morning for no apparent reason. The royal physician soon confirmed she was pregnant. Phillip was elated at the news as he had often wondered aloud if it were even possible before he started drinking the sperm enhancement mixture. When he asked his royal physician in the past, he had always been non-committal (it's possible). King Henry was especially pleased. He even made the unusual gesture of hugging Ana when her pregnancy was announced at a routine council meeting. Phillip was surprised as he had never seen his father publicly hug anyone, not even his mother, the queen.

Captain Long was not aware of Ana's pregnancy when she contacted her about being her Maid of Honor as they had just set a date. Luckily the date was near and would not interfere with her own delivery.

Word gradually got out and Ana and Phillip finally made an announcement of Ana's pregnancy. She and Paul were shocked a month later, when the doctor confirmed she was carrying twins (a boy and a girl).

Ana traveled to Houston to help Long prepare for her wedding. She was surprised that Arun wanted a traditional Hindu Indian wedding and Long, who had just wanted a quiet and simple ceremony, had surprisingly agreed (he now owed her big time). Now, they just had to find people who could help them pull it off. Arun had a lot of Indian music recordings and some appropriate clothing, but not nearly enough for the wedding party. Where could they find that?

Ana contacted the base encampment now in North America that had moved from India to see if they had made any local contacts that might cooperate in helping with the wedding – even though this was one of the original Asian sites that refused to negotiate a peace agreement. Perhaps their contacts would consider a trade of wedding materials in exchange for food or something else?

Long and Arun traveled to the former site and with suitable guards met with several locals who were willing to meet and discuss their wedding needs. The offer of quality prepper food was eagerly accepted, and merchants soon provided them with enough clothing and decorations for a traditional wedding.

Long went along with everything, even with some dance lessons for the wedding party. Ana opted out of the dance lessons as her doctor had limited her from doing anything stressful.

Ana helped Long with the wedding invitations and Long was surprised when Prince Phillip and Paul Mainer accepted invitations to the wedding. Many of Arun's former resistance members were also happy to attend. Many people in the Houston encampment now knew Long and were also happy to accept invitations. There could be more people attending this wedding than Ana and Phillip's wedding.

The big day arrived, and a scout ship transported all of Arun's friends to a large open area in the Houston encampment that had been suitably decorated for the wedding. Ana laughed when she saw James and Bill from the New York negotiations escorting two of Long's female friends during the ceremony.

Few people had ever seen a traditional Hindu wedding and were delighted with the music, the dancing, and the ceremony. After the ceremony, Ana pulled Long aside and told her in confidence about the sperm enhancing formula for Tribani males and forwarded the female health specialist's contact information to Long's tablet suggesting she ask if there were anything similar that could be done for Tribani females. Long thanked her profusely and went off to discuss it with Arun. Ana felt tired and hugged Long and Arun before she and Paul retired to a prepared guest room in the ship.

Chapter 49

CULTURAL EXCHANGES

na still had six months until her due date when her doctor strongly recommended she avoid stressful situations and traveling as much as possible to avoid potential complications as a child (and especially twins) of human and Tribani parents had never been born.

During this time, she decided to try and preserve as much as possible of the former human culture that was in danger of becoming extinct. She used the watercolor set and canvases that Arun had given her and painted portraits of Phillip and Paul as an example of what she was trying to preserve. She also reminded them of the music and dancing they had seen at her own wedding and Long and Arun's wedding as examples of cultural activities.

Phillip and Paul and the rest of the Advisory Council became strong supporters of her efforts and she met frequently with them about establishing organizations that could help with the preservation efforts. All forms of art and music, sports and entertainment were discussed. They collectively agreed to send out explanations and invitations to everyone who had a tablet or a peace talks communicator explaining the effort. Eager respondents from many encampments and from former resistance groups soon volunteered to lead or participate in many of these activities.

These activities finally convinced Phillip and Paul to push for the completion of a world-wide communication system that, in theory, would be available at all encampments and to any group that had signed a peace agreement. It certainly would be a tremendous help in the preservation activities.

The former New York resistance leaders, James and Bill, quickly volunteered to work with the Tribanis to re-establish several art galleries and musical venues in New York for the preservation efforts. Human artists and musicians and their potential Tribani counterpoints could display their works on canvases or by live performances in the former galleries and venues.

In less than two months, dozens of respondents volunteered to refurbish swimming pools, baseball fields and other sports venues with Tribani help. Paul sent numerous inquiries to Tribanis in all the base encampments describing these efforts to see if there was any interest on their part in joining any or all of these activities.

Ana was a little overwhelmed when the suggestions for sports alone, included more than 25 types, including…

archery, athletics, badminton, baseball, basketball, boxing, chess, football, hockey, karate, skating, table tennis, volleyball, weightlifting and wrestling.

Ana was keen to re-establish Chess tournaments and championships. She soon had a significant number of interested tournament players and with Arun's help developed written guidelines for the tournament. Phillip approved the development of a chess program running on tablets that enabled participants in different encampments to play chess electronically by video. Many in-person tournaments were also scheduled when site participants claimed to have physical chess sets.

By the end of her fourth month of forced inactivity she had established over two dozen organizations that also desired to promote:

- Dancing (ballet, ballroom, opera etc.)

- Drawing, oil painting, watercolors, and other artistic crafts. ...

- Music and singing. ... (Orchestra, bands, solo and piano recitals), etc.

- Photography and filmmaking. ...

- Poetry

- Pottery and ceramics. ...

- Woodworking.

- Writing competitions in short stories and novels

Both Phillip and Paul supported her efforts to preserve these forms of human activities, and they even came up with a handful of Tribani activities they thought humans would like to learn and eventually compete in, most of which were cerebral and not physical in nature. One exception was a proposed Draeger tournament (based on timers).

By the end of her sixth month, these organizations were well underway with plans for competitions or recitals or exhibitions or even craft type fairs at dozens of encampments or at revised venues in nearby cities.

As her due date neared, several advisory council members volunteered to assume responsibilities for many of these activities to take the stress off Ana (which greatly relieved her doctor's concerns).

Chapter 50

TWINS

There was a lot of excitement in the London encampment as Ana's due date drew near. Some saw this as a positive sign for human and Tribani relationships in the future. As Ana predicted, with the removal of Tribani encampments in most of Europe and all of Asia, resistance movements in those areas faded away. A brief aerial survey in fact found little evidence of any organized human activity near the former encampments. It appeared the resistance fighters did fade away back to whatever they were doing to survive before the Tribanis landed.

In addition to the cultural preservation activities underway, there were many shared activities between the remaining Tribani encampments and locals eager to get the power and running water back. Once that was done, both sides worked to help each other in the planting of crops and to establish the planetary communication system.

The big day finally arrived and many Tribanis cheered when the news and information channel broadcast pictures of Phillip and Ana holding the twins.

Done Deal

The day Phillip had long feared arrived; his father had died overnight of complications from severe allergies. Paul and the advisory council immediately made plans to formally make Phillip the new king. They also planned a simple "state" funeral for Henry. All eyes were also on Ana now, as she would now be the new queen.

Paul didn't object when Ana asked that Captain Long be the new site security leader for the London encampment. Long became the first Captain to be promoted to Colonel, a position that put her in charge of security for England and Europe (Paris and Berlin). Arun accompanied Colonel Long to London and was named as a global liaison for all issues brought up by the former resistance leaders as the agreements entered into their final stages.

Now that negotiations were finally complete (fifty-five sites had agreements with local resistance movements and all hostilities had ended), Phillip asked Ana what she wanted as this had been the subject of her first negotiation with him. She was rocking their twins to sleep and replied she already had it (their spacious home, their relationship and their boy and girl twins).

The End